SHOES IN THE RIVER

The Story of "Feather"

By Madelyn Rohrer

ISBN 978-1-7338694-5-4

Cover design: Jerry Paulsen
www.designs.jerrypaulsen.com

Thank you to my proofreaders and others who have contributed to this book: Betty Calliham, Dr. William Flanary, Victoria Ingalls, Saundra Kelley, Pastor Karen Lane, Carole Marks, Jerry Paulsen, Randy Still, and the Reverend Dr. Bradley Scott.

Introduction

"If you dig that hole any deeper, it's going to come out in China!"

"Finish your dinner. People in China are starving!"

Many of us remember those classic admonitions. As a child, I had a vision of a Chinese family sitting in their yard and being surprised by a shovel popping up out of the ground next to them. In reality, if someone in the United States could actually dig a hole deep enough to go all the way through the earth, it *would* come out in China. It truly is on the opposite side of the world from the United States.

As for people in China starving, that is also true. Up until the 1960's, the Chinese government encouraged large families, expounding the theory that population growth empowered the country by contributing to its workforce and army. While it was true in those respects, the downside was devastating – the country could not feed its people. As the population grew from 540 million in 1949 to almost a billion in 1979, famine caused widespread starvation.

The one-child-per-family edict of 1980 was a desperate measure intended to stem and ultimately reverse the problem of overpopulation. Starting in the latter part of 2013, the policy was eased considerably, but not without leaving deep scars on China and the rest of the world.

"Shoes in the River" is the story of a fictional Chinese family caught up in the lingering policies of old regimes, edicts of new regimes, and the continuing struggle for basic human rights, including freedom of worship and the freedom to embrace or reject modern technology.

While the characters are fictional, the issues are real, based on recognized and widely published historical facts. China has always been a country steeped in tradition and mystery and the keeper of veiled stories, but in more recent times has become an increasingly prominent player in some of the most important aspects of life on this planet – business and industry, commerce, international relations, and the environment.

I hope you enjoy "Shoes in the River," a single story of historical significance over a thirty-two-year time span in semi-rural China.

Madelyn Rohrer

Table of Contents

Chapter 1: Letting Go

1972 - 1992

Su-Li Ming sat on a bench next to the river and watched with sad envy as a middle-aged couple stood at the river's edge. The woman removed her shoes and threw them, one at a time, far out into the water. The man placed another pair in front of her and smiled as she slipped into them. They walked away together, obviously happy. It was a tradition understood by Su-Li, but one that she and her husband, Cheng, would never experience.

It was an old tradition. When a heavy burden was lifted from a person's shoulders – a burden that prevented someone from being happy or enjoying life, the person would throw their shoes that carried the burden into the river and put on new shoes of happiness.

Su-Li knew her burden could never be lifted; she would never be able to throw her shoes into the river and put on new ones. Her burden felt just as heavy today as it had for years...two children forcefully taken from her at birth – a son and a daughter. Chilling memories continued to haunt her, casting a shadow over any possibility of happiness, blurring the good memories of earlier years.

Watching the unexpected scene of the couple at the river rekindled thoughts, playing out before her like clips from an old

1

movie. As hard as she tried to forget the past, her mind continually pulled her back through a time warp...this time, back sixteen years to 1976.

It was a year of happiness and love. She and Cheng were young, barely in their twenties, graduated from the university, and celebrating the fourth year of their married life. It was the year they welcomed their son, Qiang, into the world...that world filled with the energy of youth and anticipation of an exciting future together as a family.

Su-Li thought about Cheng, her devoted husband; her strength when endurance failed her. A loving and attentive father, he spent time with Qiang every evening when he returned home from work, from the day Qiang was born right up to today. It was always a special bonding time for father and son.

It was Cheng who first noticed Qiang's hair. "Su-Li Pu! Have you noticed the tiny white hairs on the side of Qiang's head? He is going to have your hair!"

Cheng often called her Su-Li Pu, or sometimes just "Pu," for "feather." She had a prominent swatch of white hair on the right side of her head. When brushed back into her thick, slightly wavy black hair, it looked like she had adorned her head with a feather. She smiled, remembering how Cheng often referred to her as his "beautiful feather bride," and still did.

No, she hadn't noticed the short white hairs on the side of Qiang's head until Cheng pointed them out to her, but he was right. Qiang's hair did grow in almost exactly like hers with the distinctive "feather," only slightly narrower.

It was also Cheng who noticed how young Qiang quietly rocked his little body back and forth soon after he learned to sit up, keeping time to the beat of his mother's music.

She thought about her music. It was a big part of their lives back then, with sweet and joyful sounds filling their home.

"Maybe he will also inherit your musical talent, Pu. Maybe he will not only look like you, but will sound like you."

Musical talent! She thought about her beautiful musical instruments sitting in the back of their storage space, untouched for years. A pang of guilt tugged at her when she heard someone else playing and noticed the brief wistful look in Cheng's eyes. He loved her music and often sang along with his rich tenor voice as she played.

Su-Li was thankful for her "gift" of music. Her natural musical ability allowed her to play many instruments without taking lessons. Playing a musical instrument was more than a source of enjoyment for her; it was soothing. Plus, it was how she and Cheng first met in 1972. It was at a crowded indoor festival at the university in Beijing. Everyone was talking about the American President Nixon visiting China, optimistically anticipating a change that might allow for more freedoms. She was with a group of female students who were playing traditional Chinese instruments when an impromptu chorus of male students joined them in song. That was when she first noticed the young man with the beautiful smile and strong voice and *somehow* knew he was noticing her.

More guilt gnawed at her every time she thought about Cheng's observation of their chubby little toddler. He *did* show musical promise even before he learned the skill of walking without falling.

He joined in the happy sounds by bouncing up and down to the beat of the music while hanging onto a chair for support. He often added his own tiny voice to the chorus with made-up words sounding something like "yubby yabba dooba." They never did figure out what he was trying to say. When the music stopped, he would clap his hands and laugh and continue on his way around the table, going from chair to chair.

Such a wonderful memory...but fleeting. Her heart grew heavy again as she sat alone by the river, admitting her failure as a mother. It was the same sadness that settled over her every time she thought about Qiang's musical promise and how it was stifled at a time in his life when it should have been encouraged. It was her fault, she knew, but try as she might, she could no longer enjoy the sounds of happiness from music. It made her feel worse.

It was a constant struggle to turn off the memories...and she tried so hard! They just kept coming back – the same old movie, spilling the scenes of her life in random disorder on the floor, waiting to be picked up and reassembled so they could spill out all over again the moment she allowed her mind to wander.

Now here was the one she dreaded the most...the one that started it all, staring her in the face once again without compassion – the "year of change." Chills permeated her body as she recalled the events from then to now.

It was 1980. Qiang was four. The governor of their province informed them of a new edict limiting each family to one child. Subsequent children were now forbidden. Any children over the allowed one-per-family would be taken from the parents and sent to an orphanage to be adopted by couples who had no children.

"It is a necessary law," their governor announced – "a way of reducing the overpopulation of our country. It is being proclaimed throughout China so our government can provide sufficient food, housing, and other necessities for our people."

She was frightened at first when she thought about the impact the new edict might have on her and Cheng. They were expecting their second child in two months – surely, they would be given an exemption. But their petition fell on deaf ears. It was the law, and their governor was strict on enforcing the law, granting exceptions only if certain criteria were met. They were told they would be allowed to keep their second child if their first one was physically or mentally disabled, but Qiang was healthy and extremely bright.

The other allowable exception would be if they had enough money to pay the "additional child tax." Cheng was an accountant for a large import/export company and very good with balance sheets, estimates, and costs. He explored every way he could think of to possibly pay the tax, but even with his good salary, it would still be many times what he could make in an entire year. It was beyond their ability to pay.

Their second son, Syaran, was pulled from Su-Li's arms just minutes after he was born. It was devastating...and there was nothing they could do. Cheng held tightly to Su-Li as she sobbed at the abduction of her son, supposedly to be delivered to a childless couple in another province. They were not allowed to know who or where the other couple was. If there was anything at all to be thankful for, they came to accept with time, it was that he was a boy and not a girl. At least he had a chance for survival and a home *somewhere.*

###

Time would expose the tragic reality and dire consequences of the well-intended edict meant to solve the dilemmas of an overpopulated country.

But "time," supposedly the healer of all wounds, didn't help Cheng and Su-Li. They found themselves caught up in a movement they were powerless to control and struggled to understand. They could only watch year after year as the "new tradition" evolved.

Old tradition was the preference of male children over female children. It was always that way. Cheng and Su-Li both grew up in families that understood and accepted that thinking. Sons could carry on the family line, earn a living, and be able to provide for parents in their old age. Daughters could do none of those things. Once married, a daughter was obligated solely to her husband's family, not the one of her birth. Therefore, a daughter was considered a burden to her birth family, sometimes even "useless."

Cheng was an only child so he understood at an early age the importance placed upon him.

Su-Li had two brothers and a sister. She understood her "unimportance."

But since the one-child-per-family law of 1980 was mandated, those "old tradition" values intensified, raising the pedestal for a son even higher. Being allowed only one child, every couple wanted a son to carry on the lineage of their family, whether they brought him into the world themselves or acquired him through adoption. A daughter was a disappointment – shunned, readily given up, or simply "disposed of" so they could try again for a son. Soon the orphanages were filled to capacity with girls who were unlikely candidates for adoption, at least within China. Male children lingering in orphanages were those born with mental or physical defects, labeled "imperfect," and also unlikely to be adopted.

Timing. Su-Li blamed a lot of what happened to them on timing. *Why didn't we get married sooner? Why didn't we have Qiang sooner? Why didn't we have Syaran sooner – before the hated edict? What happened to our dreams? Why couldn't we have the family we planned and wanted?* **Where was God?!**

Anger and tears melted together as Su-Li stared out at the disinterested flowing river at the edge of her rural village. This was the exact place where she and Cheng sat years ago when they first talked about marriage and their plans. It was the same day Cheng asked her father for permission to marry his daughter. They talked about a lot of things that day...finishing their education, jobs, a home, and children. ***It was before the hated edict, she recalled bitterly!***

Even though Cheng and Su-Li both knew the importance their culture placed on having sons, they decided they would welcome, love, and nurture *all* of their children, whether they were sons or daughters. It was the first "strength" Su-Li recognized and admired in her husband-to-be, instilled in him by his faith.

Cheng was a Christian; a word Su-Li had heard but didn't know much about before she met him. Ever since Cheng's conversion to Christianity during his first year of college, he grew continually stronger in his faith. He shared his beliefs with her, especially that love was forever – love for his wife and children would be true and unconditional.

Su-Li remembered the first time she attended Cheng's underground church. It was so different from the religion that she knew...the religion she was born into. The Christian church was much more casual; it was deeply personal...*so real*. Months later, with Cheng at her side, she was baptized into the Christian faith and eager to learn more about her newly adopted "religion of choice" and its gospel. She knew she couldn't tell her parents; they wouldn't agree. Her father worked for a business near Beijing that had a lot of contracts with the government. Government workers could not have "a religion," as it was considered in conflict with their loyalties to the country. The closest her father could safely get to any religion without putting his job in jeopardy was the one he inherited from his parents – Buddhism, an ancient but still relatively approved Chinese religion.

A year later, Cheng and Su-Li married twice – once in a traditional Chinese ceremony for the sake of their parents, and again quietly in the Christian church.

No, they never could have foreseen or ever imagined the events that would soon affect their lives and change all of their young plans and dreams. It wasn't God's fault. She apologized silently to God for her angry thoughts and once again thanked Him for the blessing of her son, Qiang. But she would never stop thinking about Syaran. She held steadfastly to his memory now for twelve years – and to the hope that *someday...somehow*, he would come back to them.

Again, her movie fast-forwarded, still out of control, stopping four years later at another devastating time in her life – 1984. Why couldn't she let this horrible hurt go? Why couldn't it at least ease up? Maybe it was because *unlike the loss of Syaran, this time there was no hope for recovery or being reunited...ever.* There was nothing to pray for except peace. As hard as she prayed for peace, however, it would not come.

1984. Qiang was eight years old, an energetic and inquisitive young boy who required more and more of their attention. He did well in school, played sports, sang beautifully in their church, and brought increasing joy to Cheng and Su-Li. As they became involved in all of his activities, a fragile happiness was beginning to take root in their lives once again. The sadness Cheng and Su-Li felt after the loss of Syaran was gradually diminishing with the boyish antics and enjoyable times of the present with Qiang...until they were dealt another crushing blow.

Su-Li and Cheng learned they were expecting their third child.

She recalled the stabbing pain in her heart that day, facing the cold reality that her child...her "forbidden" child would again be taken from her as soon as it was born. At first, she thought about running away and hiding, even traveling to another country, but eventually realized the futility of such an idea. Where would she and her baby go? How would they survive? Others had tried and failed, she knew, only to be brought back to face the inevitable separation. No, running away was not the answer. It would only result in agony for her and further distress for Cheng and Qiang.

Pleading to the governor would be useless. The edict had been in effect for four years and was already being touted a success by the Chinese government, but the people knew better. The absence of young children in their village was becoming obvious, especially the absence of little girls.

Even for couples having their first child, the element of happiness was missing as there were few who were willing to join in the excitement of the once-blessed event until the gender of the child was known. That was the only thing that mattered. Until then, there was no joy...only tension. If it was a boy, *then* there would be happiness and celebration. If it was a girl, there *might* be happiness...or there might be death. Daughters were simply "disappearing."

One thing was certain – the local orphanages were overcrowded with girls, and adoptive parents desiring daughters were scarce. Su-Li and Cheng had no choice except to hope for a son and the possibility of adoptive parents.

But they couldn't help thinking about the alternative – a daughter! What would they do if they had a daughter? What *could* they do? Everyone knew the inevitable fate of daughters, whether they agreed with it or not... and surprisingly, many did! Some believed that disposing of female children was the right thing to do for the good of the country. It became common practice to place baby girls out in the elements to perish, especially if it was winter, or toss them into a ravine or down a well to die.

It was an excruciatingly sad time for parents, children, and families...until Guang made everything "easier."

Guang – *the hated one!* – *the child executioner!* Just the thought of Guang made Su-Li's heart race with pent-up anger. Oh, how many times people in their village watched him take a newborn girl child from her parents and make his way to the top of a tall hill north of the village and drop it off a cliff into the deep ravine below. It was rumored that Guang was personally appointed by the governor to enforce the one-child-per-family edict, and he was obviously loyal to the governor. The villagers surmised he was chosen for this service because of his size. He was the tallest and strongest of all the men and carried out his duty quickly, without expression – without any sign of compassion or remorse. His bulky figure could easily be seen against the sky as he made his way up to the top of the hill and to the edge of the cliff, throwing the child over the edge, and then coming back down empty handed. It never seemed to bother him how deeply he was hated by everyone. He had no family except for his mother, Mulan. She was a quiet and pleasant lady, but also despised because of her son.

So whether their child was a son or daughter, Su-Li and Cheng already knew they would have no more than a few minutes to share their joy before Guang carried it off to an orphanage and eventually to another province – maybe to another country...or to the top of the cliff!

How she hated Guang! She felt sorry for Mulan at one time, but not anymore – not since the first time she saw Guang with her own eyes carrying a child up that hill and coming down empty-handed. She shivered as she thought about that scene. *Could Mulan not make him stop? Did she even try? How could anyone be as unfeeling as Guang? – so cold and callous. How could even the most hardhearted person not have feeling for the cries of a mother being denied a child she had waited so patiently to see? And what about the child that was taken away from the love of its mother? Was Guang made of stone?*

It made no difference anyway, she told herself over and over; he wasn't going to change. Mulan wasn't going to interfere in her son's life. The edict wasn't going to go away. There was nothing she or Cheng could do or say that was going to make a difference. They prayed for God to spare their unborn child. That was all they could do.

The memories of the birth of her third child were still vivid. It was late in the afternoon and Guang was already stationed outside their door. How did he know? Who could have told him?

She knew Cheng's heart was breaking also, but there was nothing he could do except console his wife as best he could. Su-Li made him promise he would let her hold her child long enough to give it an appropriate name and then as long as he could before having to hand it over to Guang. She hoped for a son so he might live, but secretly she wanted a daughter...to keep.

Su-Li cherished every second she was able to hold her beautiful, perfect daughter. She decided to call her Xiu-Su – "beautiful and unadorned." But when Xiu-Su half wrapped her tiny hand around Su-Li's little finger, the bond between mother and daughter was sealed and Su-Li was <u>not</u> willing to let her daughter go. She refused!

"Su-Li, it is time," said Cheng softly as he tried to take Xiu-Su.

"No, no! Please! Just a few more minutes!"

She held tightly to her precious bundle, refusing to hand her over. Cheng's eyes filled with tears as he tried to take the child and comfort his wife at the same time. She held her daughter in an iron grip and closed her eyes!

"God, please don't let them take my child!"

She heard people outside the door. Suddenly many hands were holding her as Xiu-Su was pried away. Her cries turned to screams. Her head was spinning. She vaguely remembered her eight-year-old son, Qiang, frightened by hearing her frantic voice, running into the room to help and hollering "mama!" – only to be moved firmly aside by his father's arm.

Then she was left to the supporting embraces of her sister and sisters-in-law, but was not comforted. After a while, she pulled herself away and looked out the window. There was Guang's outline against the setting sun, almost to the top of the hill. She watched him throw his bundle over the edge and come back down, holding nothing.

_"No! No!"_ she sobbed as she fell back into her bed.

"Why, God? Why?"

That was the last she remembered as she lapsed into feverish despair, not caring if she lived or died.

Time did nothing to ease Su-Li's grief. She not only lost her child, but her very heart and soul as well. Cheng and Qiang did everything they could to comfort her day after day, year after year, but from then until now, there was no happiness in their home. There was no more music, singing, or laughter...just memories.

No, she would never be able to lift the burden from her shoulders, throw her shoes in the river, and put on new ones of happiness. She picked up the basket of food she purchased from the market and walked home.

It was the night of their weekly Bible meeting at the house church. It was a much smaller version of the underground church she and Cheng attended as students in Beijing, but she did not feel like going. The missionary family she knew and liked for years was returning to their own country and they were supposed to be introduced to their replacements – a husband and wife and *two children*. Even though she enjoyed her new Christian life and always looked forward to learning more of the gospel, tonight she just wanted to stay home, preferably alone. Reliving those painful memories at the river took its toll on her again. She knew Christians were supposed to be able to let go of hurt and sorrow from the past, but she just couldn't forget. She couldn't let go of the memories. After all these years, it was still raw.

But Cheng and Qiang encouraged her to join them. "I have met the new man," coaxed Qiang. "His name is Roberto. I am told that he is speaking tonight about lost children...forbidden children. It is a message of hope."

"Hope?!" That word almost made her want to lash out in anger, but she knew Qiang meant well. That word did not fit into Su-Li's life; she had no "hope!" What could this man possibly be talking about to her and Cheng or any of the other villagers who had been denied their children? It made her all the more determined not to go. It would just be another message about giving all her burdens

14

to God and looking to the future, and she didn't want to hear it. But Cheng insisted and, as always, she *wanted* to be a good wife and mother. She *tried hard* to be! Ultimately, she abided by the wishes of her husband and son.

Her first impression of Roberto and Elena was not as she expected. Their presence was somewhat comforting...especially after she learned that they also lost a child shortly after birth, although theirs was due to unforeseen complications. *They did not seem sad!* Though they mourned the loss of their child, they said they would see her again in Heaven.

Su-Li was stunned by the message. It was so simple – one she had heard before but never thought much about its true meaning. Heaven! We WILL meet again in Heaven!

Roberto's words spoke directly to her aching heart:

"We as Christians know that when we leave this world, we will go to Heaven and live eternally in that perfect place. **There we will be recognized and greeted by the loved ones who have gone on before us**...and there we will wait to greet the loved ones who will come through Heaven's gate after us. **We will be reunited** with our children, parents, and all the others whom we have loved in our lives. *You* will be reunited with your lost children in a beautiful world where there is happiness, peace and love. Yes, your children will know you and you will know them. Love is forever and cannot be taken away!

"Through the timeless lessons in the Bible, the words of Jesus himself, and the strength of our faith, we know these things to be true."

A surge of electricity went through Su-Li as she sat almost glued to her seat. It felt like a door had just burst open. When the meeting was over, she didn't want to leave. She sat right where she was and insisted that Cheng and Qiang do the same until everyone else was gone and the three of them had time to talk with Roberto and Elena alone. Elena held her hand as Roberto explained more about Heaven and let Su-Li pour out all the bitterness, pain, hurt, and feelings of abandonment that were pent up inside of her. It was the first time in years she felt any kind of relief. She held nothing back. She breathed deeply...and cried! Then she smiled. Cheng and Qiang smiled with her and also breathed sighs of relief, feeling that gloom was possibly being lifted from their lives. Cheng thanked the new leader for his powerful sermon, took the hand of his beautiful Su-Li and led her home, hoping that happiness might be returning to his family.

Chapter 2: Guang

1992 - 1994

Su-Li loved her new Christian life now more than ever. She acquired a voracious appetite for learning more of the gospel, especially now that she had her very own Chinese/American version of the New Testament, a gift from Elena. Until now, she only had access to a shared Bible.

Music came back into her life. She found herself humming an old song one day while working around the house and thought about her neglected musical instruments. She pulled them out of their small storage space and cleaned them off. How did her erhu get such a scratch on the front? How did the string on her pipa get broken? She always took such good care of all her instruments! Well, it was probably from getting pushed back into the crowded storage area over the years, she realized. At least her chimes appeared unscathed. A new string, a little tuning, hits and misses and sore fingers, and the house was filled with their sweet sounds once again. Cheng's voice was still strong and rich although it did crackle once in a while from lack of use.

And Qiang! They were surprised to hear his beautiful maturing voice as he chimed in to sing along with his father. They heard him sing many times in a church group with other teenagers, and he probably sang in school or maybe out with his friends, they realized, but he hadn't sung at home since he was a young child.

It was definitely a happy time once again for their family. They decided to share their music with the Bible study class of their underground church, much to the delight of Roberto and Elena. Others started joining them with instruments and singing. It spread to their Sunday worship services. Hymns, praise songs, and rejoicing were taken to a whole new level within their house church. "Music" could also be used if necessary to explain a reason for their meetings if they were discovered and questioned by government officials.

But with all of the wonderful revelations of her growing Christian faith, there were two things that Su-Li was *not willing* to accept...she just couldn't!

"Love" and "Guang" did not go together. Neither did "forgiveness" and "Guang." As hard as she tried to change her thinking, Su-Li knew, in all truthfulness to herself, there was absolutely no way she could forgive the person who carried off babies and cold-heartedly murdered her daughter! Even less feasible was any possible outward or inward seed of love for the man she despised down to the depths of her soul. She couldn't bring herself to even look at him when their paths crossed. The man was evil and not worthy of forgiveness! And now she was supposed to make peace with him? She refused to consider it, although Cheng and Qiang said they did forgive him.

Qiang tried to reason with his mother that she could love someone as a child of God, but not really like what he does as a person. It didn't make any sense to her and she refused to budge when it came to Guang – and she wasn't particularly impressed with his mother either. She couldn't bring herself to speak one word – kind or unkind, to Mulan, even when the woman wished her good morning or a good day. How could that woman dare to wish her a good day when her son made years of tear-filled days for her? And it wasn't just Su-Li. Other women in the village who had a child pulled from their arms felt the same way. No – love and forgiveness would not be offered for Guang!

Finally, through patient encouragement from her husband and son, teachings from the Bible, and recognizing the kindness of Roberto and Elena towards those who led sinful lives, Su-Li decided to at least pray for the softening of her heart. She didn't expect it to actually happen, but it was the right thing to do. And it did make her feel better. Hatred gradually turned to bitterness; bitterness to sadness; sadness to acceptance of God's timing, and ultimately a semi-peace...until the night she saw Guang again making his trek up the hill with a child in his arms and coming down empty-handed. Then the process took a giant step backward and had to start all over again. But this time she had someone to talk to who understood her deep-seated feelings toward Guang – Elena. Together they prayed for the lives of all of China's forbidden children and for Guang's repentance and salvation. Still, she could not bring herself to come face to face with Guang and speak words of peace between them.

Anxiety was in the air. It was a day of mixed emotions when people in the village learned that Guang had suffered a heart attack and was not expected to survive. If Su-Li's Christian life was ever going to allow forgiveness for the man, it had to be now. But she wasn't ready. She was not ready to tell him face to face that she forgave him because she didn't...not really. How could she say those words when she didn't mean them? She felt like a failure – a hidden disgrace to her church. What she did not realize until now, however, was that there were others who felt the same as she did...unforgiving.

Initially there were no tears of sorrow for Guang from anyone in the village. As days passed, however, some of those who had converted to the Christian faith visited him as a gesture of compassion and yes, even forgiveness. It was a time of moving forward, out of a dark era in their village's history. Those who did visit Guang and forgave him said that they felt a sense of relief. Many walked down to the edge of the river and, in the old Chinese tradition, threw their shoes into the water as a symbol of ridding themselves of the burden and putting on new shoes to *hopefully* walk into a better life in the future.

Su-Li could not do it, even though Cheng and Qiang encouraged her as a Christian to try. Her heart lurched as she recalled the feeling of Xiu-Su's tiny hand wrapped around her little finger and the pain of their separation. She knew she could not look into Guang's face, no matter how ill he was, and tell him with even a shred of truthfulness that she forgave him. She went quietly into her bedroom, closed the door behind her, knelt down, and prayed.

"Dear Lord Jesus, please help me. I know what I am supposed to do and how I am supposed to feel as a child of God, but I cannot help myself. You know I have tried! Why does my heart still feel angry? How can Cheng and Qiang find forgiveness and I cannot? I want to be a good person and go to Heaven someday and be with my children. Please help me find the way. I cannot do it by myself."

GUANG: 1992-1994

Life was slipping away for Guang, and although he was comforted and surprised by the number of people who came to see him off on his journey to another world, there was one person he especially wanted to talk to who had not come – a person he personally wanted to apologize to – Su-Li Ming. He remembered well the night her husband, Cheng, with tears spilling from his eyes, obediently placed the newborn child in his arms...and the young boy at his side staring up at him, watching his father hand the baby over and then rushing back into the house. He remembered Su-Li's screams of anguish behind him and how he wished he could turn around and take the child back to her - but he could not. He did what he had to do, although his heart was breaking for Su-Li and her family. She was not like many of the women who gave birth to daughters and then willingly handed them over to be destroyed so they could wait for sons.

He wished she would come by so he could talk to her and tell her his story. Maybe his mother would be willing to go to her and beg her to come to his bedside. Would she come? He knew Su-Li shunned his mother as she did him.

"Yes, I will try," his mother agreed.

Su-Li was so surprised to see Mulan at her door that she almost forgot how much she disliked the woman just because of who she was. But her innate sense of hospitality dictated that she invite Mulan into her home and serve her tea. She was equally surprised to hear that Guang had personally asked for her visit. Maybe this was God's answer to her prayer, she thought. Maybe He was helping her to move on. Yes, she would go with Mulan to visit Guang.

Guang was ashen when they arrived; his breathing was shallow and labored. Su-Li felt a small pang of pity, but it dissipated quickly. *He never showed any remorse about the breath of my daughter being snuffed out,* she thought bitterly! No, she still could not say the word "forgive."

She gazed down at the man whose face she had not been able to look at for ten years. She felt her throat tighten as she started to speak. Her words were raspy.

"I wish you well on your journey, Guang," was all she could manage to say.

She was totally unprepared for his response:

"Your daughter lives, Su-Li."

His words were like a sword through her heart. She froze and turned away in anger. How cruel! She had watched him with her own eyes as he walked up the hill, threw her child over the cliff, and came back down empty handed. Did he think she was stupid or blind? She wanted to lash out at him for his words, but she took a deep breath, turned back around, and looked straight into Guang's face.

"How can you speak such a lie on your dying bed, Guang? Did you think I was so overwrought with grief that I could not distinguish your silhouette against the sky as you took my daughter up the hill and dropped her to her death? How could you still, even now, be so cruel?!"

"I heard your cries, Su-Li, and they went deep into my heart. I wanted to tell you about your daughter for all these years but could not. Now I believe I can, for you have a right to know. Your daughter does live, and so do all the other children that I carried up the hill. What I dropped into the ravine were animal bones and rocks, handed to me from the hidden entrance of a cave near the top. I exchanged the children for animal bones and rocks. The children live."

Su-Li's mind was reeling as she tried desperately to make sense of what Guang just said. Is *he delusional? Could he possibly be telling the truth? Could my daughter really be alive?* Doubt hung heavily over the man lying before her. She had a battery of questions. *Why should I believe him? If he is telling the truth, who took the children from him and gave him bones and rocks? Who took care of the children? Where did they go? Guang was never seen going back up the hill.*

"If this is true, Guang, who helped you? You could not do this without someone to help you. Who took the children from you and handed you bones and rocks? Who took care of the children?"

His eyes were closed as he spoke, his voice more labored. "There were others...and there still are, dedicated to saving the lives of the forbidden children. We all took a solemn vow of silence, even to death. That is why I could not tell you even though I wanted to. A single sentence innocently spoken to the wrong person could have meant death for many people, including the children. Even now I cannot disclose the names to you. There is one person, however, that I have permission to make known to you alone. He

23

has taken my shoes to the river this day as the burden is finally being lifted from my shoulders. Soon I will have new shoes to wear into the next world. Please go to the river. The man who takes my place sits on a bench next to the large tree at the bend. He waits for you, hoping you will come to him."

"Why me, Guang? If this is really true, why should he wait to be made known to me? And more importantly, if this is true, where is my daughter? Where can I find her? Tell me...please!"

Su-Li's words were not heard. Guang's chest was still.

"Mulan! Please! I think Guang has died."

Mulan had been sitting quietly in a far corner of the room and was already rushing to the bedside of her son. Su-Li instinctively gave her a short but comforting hug as she ran out the door and down the road to the river. Whoever was there was the person who would be able to tell her about Xiu-Su! The large tree near the bend was a favorite meeting place for people in the village – there might be more people there than one. How would she know who she was looking for?

Her heart was pounding so hard she could hardly breathe. As she approached the bend of the river, she could see the back of someone sitting alone on the bench – a man with his head down. She walked quickly, then slowed down as she approached the bench, anxiety and fear gripping her stomach. What if this was not the person? How would she explain why she walked up to him? It didn't matter; she had to know.

GUANG: 1992-1994

She took a deep breath, walked over to the man on the bench and stood in front of him. He looked up. Su-Li gasped in disbelief...

...as she looked down into the eyes of her son.

SHOES IN THE RIVER

Chapter 3: The Cave

1994

"Qiang! You?"

"Yes, Mother. Please forgive me! I wanted to tell you and Father what I have been doing for a long time but could not. I swore an oath of silence and have carried this burden with me for years. I prayed you would come here today so you would know; Guang and I agreed that you and Father should both know. We are trusting only that you will swear our oath of silence as well. Many continue to risk their lives so children can live."

Once again Su-Li's thoughts were trying to unscramble in her mind. At least she knew now that Guang told the truth. But now…she was faced with another unexpected situation – her son, who was going to be assuming the duties of the most hated man in the village!

Her thoughts switched back to her missing children. "Where is Xiu-Su? Is she really alive? Where is Syaran? Do you know? Please tell me!"

"That is the sad part, Mother. I do not know where they are. I tried to find out after I became involved with this cause and reached a level of understanding, but I am convinced that there is no way of ever locating them. The path is permanently blocked after a child is delivered. I was told by another worker that Syaran spent only a short time in an orphanage and was received by a family a long way from here, but still in China. There are no records, only a verbal report that the transaction took place and he has a good family."

Her heart fell. "And Xiu-Su?"

"All I could find out was that she lives in another country with parents who desperately wanted a baby girl and who promised to love her and raise her as their own daughter. That is the way it has been with *all* of the children, and it is the same today. We promise to ask no questions about who the new parents will be and in return they promise to ask no questions about the birth parents. They just agree to take care of the child and love her – or him as their own. So yes, Xiu-Su lives and, like the other children, we just have to be thankful that a home and parents were found for her and she is happy and well."

Su-Li sat down next to her son, hung her head and sobbed. Her emotions had run the gamut in such a short time. Her head was full of unimaginable thoughts, all crowded together, fighting for attention:

My daughter was dead; now she is alive. There was hope she could be found; now there is no hope. My daughter lives...somewhere, but I will never be able to find her. My son, Syaran, was really adopted

28

and he is living somewhere in China. Guang, the man I hated for so many years, did not kill my daughter...he saved her life. The woman Mulan is a good person, not the insensitive, uncaring person I thought she was. My son, Qiang, is the new Guang. I am now the new Mulan.

She thought about Cheng. *How will he feel about all of this? Will he be willing to take this oath of silence? We need to tell him soon. What if he...*

She felt Qiang's arm around her heaving shoulders. "Mother, do you remember the words of Roberto when you first went with us to hear him? He explained that when we die and go to Heaven to be with God, we will be met by all our loved ones who have gone on before us, and that we will wait there to greet all of our loved ones who come after us. No matter what happens to us here on this earth, our family will all be together someday in Heaven. Do you believe that? I do."

Qiang's words were semi-comforting. She sat up and wiped her face on her sleeve. In the silence that followed, she realized her son was speaking wisely. He was right. She took a few deep breaths and replied: "Yes. I know that is what Roberto said and right now, more than ever, I know that God does answer prayers. I do believe **Heaven is for real**, and what I have learned **is** the truth. It is a great comfort to know that someday I will be able to see Syaran and Xiu-Su and that they will know me and know how much I love them and have always loved them and we will all be together."

Qiang's hand patted her shoulder. "I sincerely believe in that hope...that promise, Mother. I also believe with all my heart that in the meantime, my calling is to continue doing what needs to be done to save as many of the children as possible.

"Right now, I think we need to go home and tell Father and, when you both have had a chance to think about all this and are ready, I will take you to see the cave if you would like. We call it the Cave of Forbidden Children."

"Yes, I would very much like to see the cave and I'm sure your father will also when...as you say, he has had a chance to think about all of this. Is there a good time to go there?"

"We have found that the best time is in the middle of the day when people are busy working and there is a lot of activity in the village. That is when they would not be paying much attention to us. The other time is very deep into the night when everyone is asleep – that is when we remove the children from the cave and take them away from the village."

Qiang stood, picked up Guang's big shoes, walked to the edge of the river, and threw them out into the water. Then he took his own shoes off and threw them into the water. "I have wanted to throw away these shoes of burden for a long time. It feels good to finally be able to tell you about Syaran and Xiu-Su and all of the other children from our village."

He reached into a pouch attached to his waist, took out a new pair of sandals, and put them on.

###

THE CAVE: 1994

Qiang, Cheng, and Su-Li made their way casually but steadily toward the bottom of the hill and the path leading to "the cliff" and ravine. Su-Li followed her son and husband, silently revisiting their conversation of three nights ago. Cheng reacted just as she had anticipated, with the same outward emotion of shock and then outpouring of some of the same inner emotions she felt, but with considerably more restraint. Cheng was always better at controlling his feelings than she was. It was another strength she loved and appreciated in her husband.

Of course, they agreed to the oath of silence. How could they not, without endangering the life of their son and the lives of others including the children?

Still, Qiang offered to forego further involvement in his mission if it would cause his parents anguish.

"There are others who can do the job just as well as I can," he explained. "There is no special training – just the desire and caring to be involved and peace in our hearts when we save the life of a child. I am willing to suffer for this cause just as Guang did. I know the time will soon come when I will have to endure the stares and shuns of people who once called me friend, but I cannot ask you to share in my suffering. I will do only as you wish."

Cheng and Su-Li talked long into the night. There was no question in their minds that their son was doing an admirable thing...the right thing and the only thing that could possibly be done to save children who would otherwise be killed for the simple reason of being born at the wrong time and in the wrong place. They realized and agreed that God spared their own daughter through the efforts of those who were willing to risk death to become involved. Now it was their turn to help others.

"We are proud of what you are doing, my son," said Cheng. "Your mother and I will support the cause however we can. We are ready."

As they approached the bottom of the hill, Qiang suddenly veered off to the left, away from the visible upward path they were so familiar with, as though heading for the scenic but rocky narrow ledge above the river. They were soon out of sight of the busy village. A few minutes later, Qiang turned again, taking them into a small clearing. He pushed aside some brush with his walking stick, uncovering a narrow path that looked like it was headed for a steep and uninviting area of thorny growth. Su-Li and Cheng followed their son upward, continually pushing the overgrowth out of the way with their walking sticks as he did. Before they reached the thorn bushes, however, the path turned sharply to the left, then again to the right and up the back of the hill until they were overlooking the ravine. It looked like the edge of a place no one would want to walk, seemingly disappearing into an even steeper incline of brush-covered rock.

Qiang stopped to give them all a much-needed rest, motioning to a large, sun-warmed flat rock to sit on. Cheng and Su-Li were still looking for the entrance to a cave, or at least a continuation of their uneven path. There was nothing but a rock wall in back of them, a ravine in front of them, and wilderness above.

After a minute or two, Qiang nonchalantly commented about the beautiful view overlooking the river, and added: "Do you feel the cool breeze?"

Yes, they did, but only after Qiang mentioned it. Then Cheng realized it was coming from behind them, not up from the river!

"This is how Guang discovered the cave," Qiang explained. "He was climbing the hill to enjoy what he thought would be a beautiful view on a warm day and stopped here to rest. As he sat on this rock, he was surprised by the cool breeze on his back and looked for its source. That was when he discovered a small entrance to a cave. He was curious and pulled away some of the brush so he could look in and realized the cave was actually quite large. So even after making the entrance large enough for us to walk in, I think you will agree it is still well hidden."

They both looked around. "You are right, Qiang," said Cheng, turning his face toward the breeze to search for the cave. "I know it must be over this way, but I still don't see it."

Qiang smiled and walked toward the wall of rock, several steps back from their resting place, moved some overgrowth out of the way with his stick, and pulled aside two scraggily scrub trees to allow them to enter.

There was soft daylight in the cave, filtering in from several openings high up on two of the walls, with shadows of leaves moving gracefully over them. It was not a lot of light, but enough to

33

see fairly well after they stood for a few moments to let their eyes adjust from the light of the outside.

"Have a look around," Qiang said with a chuckle. "This is where I spent many hours away from home when you thought I was just out with my friends!"

Cheng walked around the perimeter, examining the structure of the cave walls, looking into holes and crevices. "Is there just one opening?" he asked.

"There is another entrance farther up on the other side, Father, also well hidden. That is where the children are exchanged for rocks. This is the entrance the children are removed from – away from the sight of our village. As you can see, there are also a few openings on the inner wall that lead to small tunnels, but we have not attempted to explore any of them to find out where they go. We *have* met a few animals through the years that emerged from the tunnels, but they were probably more afraid of us than we were of them. This main room and the smaller one above are the only ones we occupy; they suit all of our needs.

"The small openings above us that let daylight in are so well hidden and so high that even when we are here at night and light a lantern, the light does not shine out enough that anyone would notice.

"There is also one rather unique opening on the wall over here, Father," Qiang said as he led them up the incline and pointed to a narrow fissure in one of the crevices. "This is where whoever was in the cave could sit and watch for Guang as he started up the top part of the hill. It would take him about ten minutes to get from the point where we could see him through this slit in the wall to the area of the other cave entrance. That is where we would meet him and quickly take the child in exchange for a bundle of animal bones or rocks wrapped in cloth. Guang would then walk the other way, away from the hidden entrance and toward the edge of the ravine where he would be visible to anyone who might be watching from a distance. Then, while the child was being taken back into the cave, he would ceremoniously throw his bundle over the side of the cliff. If anyone should ever follow him or come up the hill at another time and look down, it would look like a scattering of blankets and remains on the floor of the ravine."

Meanwhile, Su-Li was standing quietly in the center of the chamber, taking in the sights from her stationary position while listening to the conversation between Cheng and Qiang. She noticed that the large curved wall to her right appeared to have drawings and writings on it. She walked over to get a better look...and stopped cold when she realized what was before her. The "drawings" were tiny footprints! The writing underneath of each one was a date. Some of them had a name under the date. Their significance was obvious, and she quickly recognized they were in chronological order. Her heartbeat accelerated as she walked along the wall, instinctively searching for the date etched in her memory.

There it was! – a tiny footprint with her daughter's birthdate and the words "Xiu-Su" painted underneath.

Cheng was jolted when he heard Su-Li's cry: "Cheng!" He turned around to find her standing motionless, facing the wall.

As Cheng rushed to her side, Qiang stood quietly, knowing it was a very special time for his parents. If there remained any doubt that Xiu-Su survived that terrible night, it was now put to rest. Su-Li and Cheng stared at the wall and then clung to each other in a tearful embrace. They stood in front of the wall again, this time gingerly running their fingers over the tiny painted footprint. Su-Li's mind slipped back in time as she felt the footprint and remembered the bond that she and her daughter shared for just seconds the night Xiu-Su was born.

After a few moments of struggling to compose herself, Su-Li resumed her search along the wall; Cheng walked with her. "Qiang. I do not see Syaran's footprint here."

"No, Mother. He had an adoptive family waiting for him in another province and was transported directly to an orphanage and then to his new home a few days later. Being a healthy baby boy, there was no need to bring him here – his life was never in danger."

Healthy. For the first time, Su-Li thought about the destiny of baby boys who were born less than perfect. *Were they considered as useless and disposable as girls were,* she wondered?

"Have there been any baby boys brought here," she asked?

"Just one. He was a second child and born with a deformed right arm. Under such circumstances, his parents could have kept him, but they decided to give him up because of the deformity. He would not have been adoptable within our country, but we are thankful for compassionate people in other countries who are willing to accept imperfect children whether they are boys or girls."

Su-Li never thought about being the parent of a deformed or disabled child. For just a moment, she strangely wished it could have been so with Syaran – she would have been able to keep him! Then she felt selfish with her juxtaposed thoughts. *What kind of a mother am I that I would rather my son be born deformed than be healthy and raised by someone else?*

Her mind returned to the present and the reality of Syaran's existence in another place. She always hoped it was true that her beautiful, perfect son was adopted by a family who would love him and raise him as their own...now she knew. It was a bittersweet moment. She wanted to burst with joy, realizing that both of her lost children were alive, but the bubble of joy dissipated with the realization she would never know them.

More questions preyed on her mind: *Were they happy? Did they know they were adopted? Did they ever ask about their real parents? Maybe it made no difference. The important thing was...they lived!* She was suddenly filled with a peace she never thought would be hers - a sweet, joyous peace. She smiled, walked over to her son and hugged him.

Accepting his mother's embrace and sensing her peace, Qiang again apologized for not being able to share what he knew earlier. "I tried to think of ways I could lessen your anger, Mother, and bring you peace without having you drawn into our mission. I wanted you *both* to know, but didn't know how to tell you or how much I *could* tell you."

It was Cheng's turn to hug his son. "Qiang, thank you for bringing us here. Of course, we will tell no one of this place." Then he laughed. "We probably wouldn't be able to tell anyone where it was anyway! Let's finish looking around. What's over here in this adjoining room?"

They walked away from the entrance, around a bend in the wall and up an incline into a smaller room where there were baby supplies, a cradle filled with many layers of soft blankets, a rocking chair, lanterns, a small stove, and a single bed. "This is where the children are cared for while waiting to be moved into the system," Qiang explained. "The timing has to be right and it has to happen as quickly as possible. We cannot keep them here very long, especially if the weather is cold. Sometimes it is a matter of hours, but other times it could be days before the transporter arrives and we feel it is safe.

"During that time, the caregiver will mix up a little paint from this jar, apply it to the bottom of the baby's right foot, and put the imprint on the wall in its proper place. Then the date is applied and, if the child was named, we add it when the name becomes known, which was the case with Xiu-Su. If a child was not named, the caregiver chooses a name for the child. It just seems like the right thing to do. Then, if we need to refer to the child later, perhaps as she travels through the tunnel, she has a name.

"Of course, I cannot disclose the route that is taken from here. I only know the first part of it anyway; that is all I have traveled. That is all most of us know."

Su-Li looked through the supplies, making mental notes of nice things she could purchase to add to a baby's comfort. But how could she buy them without someone noticing? No wonder the supplies were sparse, she realized.

"Qiang, do I remember that you...or maybe it was Guang, referring to this place as the Cave of Forbidden Children?"

Qiang chuckled. "Well, we had to call it *something*, and we decided that the Cave of Forbidden Children would certainly be an appropriate name. Among ourselves, we just call it The Cave."

"Is it alright if I call it by another name?"

"What would you like to call it?"

"Well, the Cave of Forbidden Children" sounds like they are all doomed - born to die when, in fact, these children were born to live in spite of what others would do to them." She nodded toward the far wall. "Wherever those feet are, they belong to children who are very much alive and bringing happiness to many parents. Can we call this place The Cave of Happy Feet?"

"So it will be, at least among us."

As they made their way back down the camouflaged path, Su-Li thought about Mulan. *What a strong woman she must be*, she thought, *rising above the way she was treated all these years, knowing that people hated her because they hated her son.*

"Qiang, is Mulan one of the people who took care of the children while they were in the cave?"

"I'm sure I would be allowed to tell you the answer to that, Mother. Yes. During the first couple of years, Mulan was the *only* one. She and Guang had no family other than themselves, and their neighbors would not speak to them. They had no friends who knew if they were home or even cared, so they did everything themselves. Other helpers were eventually...and very carefully recruited, so Mulan did not have to be the only caregiver. Guang remained the only *visible* person, however."

"Was she the one who took care of Xiu-Su?"

"I don't know; I was not involved at that time. Would you like me to ask her?"

"No."

Chapter 4: Mulan

1994

The sun was low in the sky when they returned to the village. Su-Li hurried to fix a hot meal for her two wonderful men and made another portion of her special rice cakes to take to Mulan the next day. She wanted to spend quality time with the woman who was suddenly very important to her – a woman she scorned just days ago. It was time to ask for forgiveness.

###

It was a quiet morning; Su-Li passed no one on Mulan's road. As far as she knew, no one saw her walking to the home of the woman she publicly shunned for years. She had a scarf ready to pull over her head and face if she needed it, but it was still laying on her shoulders.

"Mulan, do you have time to spend with a foolish and rude woman?"

"You grace my home, Su-Li. Please come in."

As Mulan prepared tea, Su-Li unwrapped the cakes she brought. She looked around at Mulan's small but comfortable

41

looking home. There was a picture of Guang sitting atop a large black shellacked chest near the wall. For the first time, Su-Li *really looked* at Guang's face...the face she always saw as stoic, without compassion or feeling. It was smiling. He actually *was* a handsome man, she realized.

A strange feeling came over her – she suddenly felt unworthy of being in his house. She treated the man who rescued her daughter like an outcast, but how could she have known what really went on in his life, his home, his mind? She wished she could tell him how sorry she was. Maybe somehow he knew.

"Mulan, I have come here to apologize for the way I treated you and Guang. I didn't know about your son...or *my own son,* until a few days ago. I know that does not excuse my poor public behavior in blaming Guang for carrying out his job and for ignoring you simply because you were his mother. For ten years, I have been bitter against you for no fault of your own. Cheng and I brought a forbidden child into this world. It was our fault, not Guang's, not yours.

"And do not be concerned - Cheng and I have both taken the pledge of silence. We have been to the cave and fully support the cause for saving our children."

With their friendship reignited, the two women enjoyed each other's company well into the afternoon, almost like two schoolgirls at a class reunion. Although Mulan was a few years older than Su-Li, they had known each other since childhood. Today, however, they were both young in spirit and wise in years. It felt so good to smile and laugh, although Su-Li knew Mulan's heart must be aching terribly for her son. It was, but Mulan's concern was for Su-Li, Cheng, and Qiang. The issue at hand needed to be discussed.

"I wish I could spare you the hurt and rejection you will feel, Su-Li. You have not yet been tested, but the time will soon come. However, please know that not *everyone* will treat you poorly. Others are working for our cause and you will eventually realize who they are, but you cannot ask and you cannot assume. You can only appreciate their companionship in silence."

"I understand, and so does Cheng. We are willing to do whatever we can. We are proud of our son, as you undoubtedly were of your son, and while we do not know why he was chosen to walk in Guang's shoes, we do know the desire to be involved comes from his heart."

Mulan smiled and, after some hesitancy, decided to fill in some of the missing information for her new friend. "You have a right to be very proud of your son, Su-Li, but Qiang was not just 'chosen,' as you may think. Perhaps you and Cheng should know how Qiang really became involved. Obviously, he did not share it with you, and that does not surprise me as he takes his oath of silence seriously which, in itself, would have been reason enough to become involved as a leader.

"It was several years ago...five I believe. Guang was taking a child up the hill to safety and thought he heard a noise in back of him. He dared not approach the top of the hill near the cave if someone *was* following him so he hid in one of the rock crevices to confront whoever might be coming along in back of him.

"As suspected, someone *was* in back of him. It was a very angry thirteen-year-old boy – your son. Qiang had decided he was going to somehow put a halt to Guang's disposal of babies. He didn't want you to be sad anymore; he wanted to stop the pain caused to you and your husband. He physically tried to take the child from Guang and threatened to mobilize all of his friends to put a stop to 'the execution of our children.' He was so fired up and furious over what he thought Guang was doing that, for his own good and for the good of our cause, Guang made a decision to talk honestly to Qiang, as young as he was...or our whole operation could very well have been derailed. We were prepared to deal with government intervention, but not with that of a young village boy.

"Guang didn't show him the cave right then, of course, just assured him in a general way that the child was not going to be harmed, but he couldn't tell him more unless he accepted the oath of silence...and he did. Guang sensed that Qiang was trustworthy and was obviously loyal. He explained how it only looked like he was throwing children over the cliff, and it had to be done that way to satisfy the government mandate. He assured him the child was going to be delivered in safety to secret parents.

"Qiang is the only person we know of, by the way, who has ever actually climbed down into the ravine and poked through the pile of stones and bones. It was a dangerous thing to do, but he apparently felt he had to prove to himself that Guang was telling the truth.

"Qiang kept his promise of secrecy, convinced that if he spoke of anything he learned, it could endanger other children. That was all he was entrusted with at the time. He was a man – or child of his word. We all knew how much he wanted to ease your pain, but he proved trustworthy to the cause. We knew he kept his silence

44

because your dislike for Guang and me did not change. If you would have treated us differently, we would have known Qiang spoke to you. Little by little, he was given more information as he needed to know. He wanted to help, probably knowing or at least hoping that someday he would be able to tell you about Xiu-Su. Of course, we all hoped that day would come as well. Now it has. So, you see, no one chose Qiang; he chose us."

A wave of enlightenment swept over Su-Li as she realized the significance of what Mulan was saying. The pain she herself caused for her husband and son by not letting go of her hurt, for not trying harder to forgive, for not recognizing God's timing for all things, actually had somewhat of a meaningful role to play for all those years. In her grief, she only saw things from her own perspective – her lost children and personal sadness, how she believed she was forsaken by God, and not knowing why. Now she saw a much bigger picture in which she played only a small part. *Now...she knew* God was in control all along. He *did* answer when she called out to Him. He *was* there. He heard her.

It was almost as if Mulan was reading her mind. "Su-Li, I know this might not be much of a consolation to you for all your years of unhappiness and believing your daughter was dead, but your pain was not in vain. If you were not hurting so deeply, Qiang would not have become involved. Then there would have been no way to ever tell you your daughter was alive. You would not have been able to put peace back into your life by knowing your children were safe. Unfortunately, not all the mothers of forbidden children have resisted letting go of them like you did. More and more of our society are looking at disposal of children as a duty to our country and its population problem. We pray that someday there will be a different solution and our people will once again be able to keep and cherish their children."

More truths...more questions. Su-Li did not intend to ask the personal question that suddenly spilled out, but she had to know:

"Did you take care of Xiu-Su?"

Mulan hesitated for just a few moments before sharing with her friend what might be the only pleasant memories she would ever have of her precious daughter's first days.

"Yes, I did. She was a beautiful, perfect little girl. I remember she made a cooing sound when I painted the bottom of her foot to make a print for the wall; it must have tickled her. Or maybe it was just cold on her foot. I remember that she seemed the happiest when she was bundled up snugly and rocked. I kept her wrapped up in that pretty little blanket with pink and blue stars on it that she arrived in. She cried very little – only when she was hungry. She did have a good appetite – woke up several times during the night to be fed. She seemed very alert and happy the next day before she was taken on the journey to her new home. I know it's not much, but it is all I can remember. I hope it brings you comfort and not sadness."

There was a big lump in Su-Li's throat as she listened to her friend's recollections. No, she would never know the joys of caring for Xiu-Su, but at least Mulan's memories filled a small void in a very large blank space of knowing what her daughter was like.

"Thank you, Mulan. I will always cherish your words."

But that was the small picture, she reminded herself. The big picture was...Xiu-Su was alive!

It felt good to relax in the presence of a friend and be able to talk and listen so personally. In fact, they talked so much about Qiang, Xiu-Su, and herself that she almost forgot why she was really there – to comfort Mulan on the death of Guang and offer apologies. She took a deep breath and continued: "One other question, Mulan, and please forgive me if it is too personal. If you do not wish to answer, I will understand...it is only because I care about you."

"Ask whatever you wish."

"What are you going to do now that Guang is..."

The word "dead" stuck in her throat. She didn't know the faith of Mulan. Did she believe in Heaven and seeing loved ones again?

"Guang is only dead from this earth, Su-Li. I know that and believe it. Guang was a Christian and so am I. He died peacefully, knowing where he was going, and I know I will see him again when it is my time."

Su-Li breathed a sigh of relief for her friend as well as herself as she continued with her question. "My concern is if you will be alright without Guang. You have no husband or son to provide for you, and you are still young. Do you have means to support yourself until you become eligible for government funds? If not, perhaps

47

Cheng and I can help you. We don't have a lot, but we will share what we have."

"You are so kind, my friend. Yes, I am too young for government funds, but I will be alright until then. My husband was able to save money before he died and I have not had to use any of it because Guang was a good provider. I also have a daughter-in-law who makes a good living and we remain friends. She has pledged to continue to help me, although I did not ask it of her."

"A daughter-in-law?" Su-Li was still reeling from all of the surprises of the last few days. Nothing could *really* shock her any more, she thought, but the fact that Guang was married still made her mouth drop in amazement...and to Mulan's amusement.

"Yes. They decided to keep their marriage a secret. I am bound to honor their wishes so I cannot disclose her name, but she is a sweet girl and Guang wanted to protect her if he could from the scorn of the villagers. They met through their involvement in the children's cause and fell in love, but did not marry right away as Guang did not want her to have to endure the same ill treatment he watched me go through. I don't think he realized how scornfully people treated me until he saw it for himself. Then it was too late. But please do not misunderstand, Su-Li. I do not regret one thing about my involvement with saving the children. I would have done it anyway, with or without Guang, even if I had known what was ahead.

"So, after a couple of years, Guang and his lovely lady decided to marry. Her parents left China many years ago and there was no communication with them. It was their own decision, therefore, to marry privately in a small ceremony in our underground church.

"Guang spent his days here and most nights with his wife in their apartment at the edge of the village…the area near the market where there are many streets with apartments. It is mostly working people who live there, so no one really paid much attention to who was home and who was not. They have a small son who is the joy of my life; it is always a good day when I can visit him and his mother. He does not understand why his father is not coming home anymore. We are hoping for his own sake that time will take away the memory of his father. It is a sad thing to wish for, but it must be."

Another surprise! Guang was a father! They sat quietly for a while, for which Su-Li was grateful as she absorbed all of the latest revelations.

"Mulan, where is your church? Do you have a mission house or do you meet in a home?"

Silence and then a sigh from Mulan made Su-Li realize she had charged ahead with many questions without really thinking. Perhaps she had inquired too deeply. She didn't mean to.

"I would very much love to be able to go to a larger mission house like yours, Su-Li, but my presence…*our* presence would have been uncomfortable. Maybe someday. You and Cheng probably have not had time to think about it, but I want you to know that others will change in their treatment of you. I am sorry to tell you that people you have known as friends in the past may not look upon you kindly when it becomes known that Qiang is the new child executioner. If your church becomes uncomfortable, please let me know. Guang and I received the message of the gospel each week from a Christian family not far from here in a private home. I can arrange to have you and Cheng included as well."

"Child executioner." Those words made her shiver. She had not thought of that label being attached to her son but, of course, it would be. That is what people in the village called Guang.

She also hadn't thought about not being welcomed at their mission house...their beloved underground church. Yes, it *was* well attended and not really hidden like the smaller house churches, but no one bothered them. Maybe it was because it didn't have the markings of a church on the outside. Would they now be rejected? Would their presence put their church in danger?

Her mind was spinning once again with new thoughts: *Perhaps Cheng and I should have a private talk with Roberto and Elena. I don't want the mission house to suffer because of us, and I know Cheng will feel the same way. But I will miss our church. I will miss our friends. I will miss the music. Well, Cheng and Qiang and I will decide what to do.*

It was time to leave. "Mulan, when it becomes known that Qiang has taken Guang's place, I think it would be best for us not to be seen together. Perhaps when the attention falls on *my* house instead of yours, people will forget about you so that you may have peace and be able to spend happier times with your daughter-in-law and grandson. So if I do not pay attention to you when we pass on the street or at the market, please understand."

"Thank you, Su-Li; it will be as you wish. May Jesus who loves the children walk with you and your family."

Many burdens had been lifted from Su-Li's shoulders in a very short time. Even though she had *new concerns* about her son and his dangerous mission, as well as for the safety of her church and its members, *knowing her children were alive* gave new meaning to her own life. It was uplifting...**and it was time to shed her shoes of sadness.**

Su-Li walked to the river, threw her old shoes as far out into the water as she could, pulled new ones from her tote, and put them on her feet. She walked home wearing her new shoes.

SHOES IN THE RIVER

Chapter 5: Qiang

1994 - 1996

Qiang was late...very late. Dinner hour had come and gone and Cheng was sitting outside their door, anxiously waiting for him. A wail from somewhere deep in the village cut through the chilly air. Then silence. It was almost dark when Cheng called Su-Li to the door.

"Look up the hill," was all he said.

It was a familiar sight, but with a different silhouette against the rising moon – a slightly smaller man than they were used to seeing, walking up the hill with an arm bent forward as though carrying something, then coming down empty-handed. When Qiang returned home, his eyes were bleary. He sank down onto his large cushioned chair.

"I never knew it could be possible to feel so good and yet so bad at the same time," he said, staring into space almost as though he was talking out loud to himself. "How I wish I could have turned around and handed that baby back to her sobbing mother, but I had to stay focused on taking her to safety. It was so hard to keep all expression from my face, and the people who saw me and knew me looked shocked. I just had to keep walking fast to the hill, holding the baby next to my body for warmth. She had no clothes, just wrapped in a thin cloth and shivering. My heart hurt so much…until the caregiver met me at the top with a warm blanket. She took the baby and handed me a bundle of stones that I ceremoniously threw over the edge.

"Coming back down the hill was a strange feeling – kind of like finishing first in some kind of endurance test that would not be looked upon by others as anything good. There were a lot of cold stares as I walked through the village. I do not care for myself, but my thoughts were about you, my parents, as I walked toward home.

"It came into my mind as I saw my father waiting outside the door and the anxious looks on your faces that I cannot allow *my* mission to destroy yours. I know you share my passion for saving children, and for that I am grateful, but you both have a calling of your own with the church. I have seen how your music draws people in and makes them feel good – people who have listened and stayed and learned; people whose hearts and eyes have been opened. It is not right for my mission to hurt you and hurt the church. I know that everything our mission stands for is done with love, but I cannot show love for others and not for you. The right thing for me to do is move away from this house so I can pursue what I need to do without hurting your efforts or those of Roberto and Elena and the church."

It was the cold truth. Cheng and Su-Li both knew their son's words were wise – their music ministry *was* an important part of their church, and the church was an important part of many lives. But the thought of their only "allowed" child leaving home was heart-crushing. It was not their decision, however; Qiang had already made up his mind that this would be their last night together. Su-Li thought about last week's gospel lesson at church: **"Pick up your cross and follow me."** She and Cheng and Qiang didn't know where their roads were destined to lead, but they affirmed their commitment to follow in faith.

Emotions were high, low, scary, proud, and sad the next day when, as parents, Cheng and Su-Li watched their son walk away.

###

The news spread quickly. Within days Su-Li and Cheng felt the coolness of people who used to be friends. Neighbors did not speak to them. No one sat beside them at the mission house, much to the surprise of Roberto and Elena. Words were not spoken, but the silence was loud. Many people refused to join them for music. Their lives had unmistakably changed...*then they changed again!*

It was the third week after Qiang's first trek up the hill with a newborn baby that his absence from home and the mission house was becoming obvious. The scorn that had been directed at Cheng and Su-Li was turning to compassion and even sympathy. At first, they didn't know why people were suddenly befriending them again.

"We have heard," said one of their neighbors, "that Qiang has chosen a path that brought shame to your house and has been banished. It must have been a difficult thing for you to do; we know how you loved him and how you grieved when your other children were taken from you. He was your only son. Your hearts must be breaking."

When Cheng realized what Qiang or "someone" did or said to protect them, he could only hoarsely reply, "We will always love the son we knew." The tears of pride that welled up in his eyes were taken as tears of sadness. From that day, Cheng and Su-Li were looked upon as prominent examples of the fallacy of the one-child-per-family mandate.

Another change was an increasing wave of sentiment regarding the "idealism" of one child. A son carrying on the family line, leading a life that would make his family proud, marrying and having one child, and providing for his parents in their aging years, was not realistic. Yes, admittedly sometimes it *did* happen that way but, overall, it did not. Idealism was not reality. People were increasingly starting to speak out against the flawed system. They wanted <u>children</u>, not just one child growing up alone. And where were the young women that their sons someday should marry? Would their sons have to go outside of the country to find suitable wives? When was this hurtful mandate going to end?

People looked to Cheng and Su-Li more and more as symbols of perseverance and inspiration. They suffered the loss of all three of their children. Who will care for them in their old age? Yet they appear happy. How can this be? For those who asked, they explained Christianity, the gospel, and the "true idealism" of Heaven through hope and faith. Their attitudes, beautiful music, and caring for others shone like beacons. They were instrumental in the steady growth of their mission house, which now required two services each week...and then three.

Cheng and Su-Li were not without sadness, however. There were still days and nights when they would cringe at the anguished cry of a mother. They would look to the hill at the north and watch their son's silhouette against the sky, delivering yet another baby from impending death to caring arms and ultimately to waiting parents. But they missed Qiang. They prayed for *real* change so that he might be able to come back home.

It was a sunny day in the marketplace as Su-Li walked among the vendors, looking for the "just right" plump fish for dinner. She was startled to hear her name spoken by an unknown woman standing next to her.

"Are you Su-Li Ming?"

"Yes, I am."

"I have a message for you from Qiang. He wants to visit you tonight when the moon is high in the sky and above the clouds so there will not be much light. Is it agreeable with you that he should come? Please just quietly answer yes or no."

It was all Su-Li could do to squelch a cry of happiness! "Yes! Tell him yes!" she whispered hoarsely."

Su-Li knew the importance of lack of emotion, and she tried hard to maintain a stoic demeanor, but after the surprise encounter with a stranger, her feet hardly touched the ground. She changed the menu in her mind as she hurried along. Tonight, she would make Qiang's favorite meal; she had not seen her son in months!

Cheng hardly had one foot in the door when Su-Li flew into his arms and bubbled over with the good news.

It *was* a dark night as they waited for the sliver of a moon to rise high in the sky. They scarcely saw Qiang walking up to their door carrying...a guitar. It was a birthday gift for his mother. Su-Li knew about guitars and heard them played on occasion, but never tried one. She *did* comment at one time, however, that it looked like an "interesting" instrument. Qiang remembered and found one for her.

There were hugs, tears, and laughter as the three reunited, getting caught up on what each had been doing. Cheng told about his conversation with the neighbor, the *perception* of what had transpired among them, the position of responsibility being placed upon them in their church, growth of their music ministry, and how the church was expanding.

"Music is becoming very important in our church," Cheng added. "Other people are now bringing instruments to play and we are learning many hymns. Just as you wisely recognized, my son, it *has* become our personal mission. Now please tell us how *your* mission is progressing. How are you faring? Do you feel you are safe?"

"There will always be the danger of our operation being discovered, of course," Qiang replied. "So we are very careful not to draw attention to anyone or anything other than the supposed disposal of children and its message, meant to discourage the desire for more children. But I wish to tell you about my trip to Beijing several weeks ago. It has been on my mind that I need to tell you what I have seen.

"Because I have no one near me to know or care if I am away, I often make the journey from the cave to the first safe house, which is about one hundred and fifty kilometers from here. That is where I turn the children over to a man and two women...a husband and wife and the husband's sister. I stay overnight in their house and then the man takes the child from there to the next stop of the journey and I return home. The last time I delivered a child, he asked if I had ever been to Beijing and I told him no, but my parents lived there while attending the university. He asked if I would like to travel to Beijing with him sometime to see how the one-child mandate has affected that city. Of course I said yes, so last week I traveled with him to Beijing."

There was a long pause. It was obvious to Cheng and Su-Li that there was some deep emotion going on in Qiang that was making it difficult for him to talk. They sat quietly until he was ready to continue.

"My first impression of Beijing was that it is a beautiful city, but we did not stay in the beautiful places very long. We went to where it was not pretty...streets and narrow alleys filled with piles of rubbish. We wore old clothes like street people and poked through the rubbish as though we were looking for food or things of value. We did this for several hours the day we arrived. My friend told me this is how our people in Beijing find discarded children."

Qiang stopped once more. Su-Li placed her hand on his arm. "Would you like more tea? We could talk about this later if you would like."

"No, Mother. I will be fine. It's just that there are pictures embedded in my mind that I wish I could forget, but know I have to remember.

"Later that day, we *did* come across a baby. She was dead, wrapped in a plastic bag. Her throat had been cut. I was not prepared for that kind of brutality. I knew it was happening, but to actually see it was still a shock." He took another deep breath.

"The second day we met a woman who was doing the same thing we were, at least we think she was, but she would not talk to us. It seemed strange that she went through one of the piles so quickly, like she was looking for something in particular. She kept looking at us like she wished we would go away, so we did, but we watched secretly near the entrance to the alley where we knew she would have to come out. When she did come out, she was carrying a large bag and what was in it was moving.

"My friend told me that there are people in Beijing who search the alleys every day, listening for cries, watching for movement. They have rescued many babies who were simply put out in the street in bags or boxes like pieces of garbage. It is a different kind of rescue than the one I am involved in and, in a way, I am thankful to have seen it for myself, as gruesome as it was. And I am thankful for the street people...or those who look like street people, who are part of the effort to save these children. It has made me even more aware of how important our mission is. It has to continue until our society changes and families become important again. Something has got to change!"

His eyes glistened with tears as he turned his head away from his parents. After a few moments of silence, Cheng asked, "Are you going back to Beijing, son?"

He turned back to face his father. "No. I am told that there is already an extensive group of workers in Beijing. I am needed here."

The hour was late and Qiang was obviously tired. Su-Li encouraged him to stay and sleep in his own bed for the rest of the night and as long as he wished into the day, suggesting he could leave again the next night under cover of darkness. He gladly accepted the invitation.

It was good to be able to cook for her son again, and so comforting to have him home!

Qiang awoke late the next morning to the wonderful aroma of his mother's cooking and soft "plunks" on her new guitar.

"Listen, Qiang. Do you recognize this song?"

"Yes, I do, Mother. You used to sing it to me when I was young."

Qiang sang quietly as his mother played "Yes, Jesus Loves Me," awkwardly, but steadily plunking and strumming. He smiled, knowing that he definitely chose the right gift for her birthday.

It was several hours after dinner when Qiang decided it was dark enough for him to disappear into the night. With hugs, well wishes, and a promise to return soon, he was gone. It was now up to Cheng to listen or sing along with Su-Li as she plodded her way through trial and error on this new instrument that was made in America...in a place called Tennessee.

Chapter 6: A New Home

1996 - 1998

Cheng and Su-Li were two of a small handful of people whom Roberto and Elena considered "staff" at their church...they were *officially* in charge of the music program. The other staff members included Yi Ze, an interpreter who assisted Roberto with services in Chinese, Da-Biao, who prepared the room for communion and baptisms and straightened up after each service, Nuo, a woman in charge of Bible stories for children, and Tai and Jian, who were assigned the task of looking for a larger meeting place for their growing congregation.

After a thorough search of the area, Tai and Jian now had three options ready to be discussed; Roberto called a staff meeting.

The first possibility was a vacant building in the busiest and most populated area of the village. It would undoubtedly draw more people into their church because of its location but, in turn, the good location could also present a higher risk of being discovered. The front side looked like it might have been a row of adjoining stores at one time. For the sake of security, they decided that the stores would have to be re-established as working businesses – run by their members, of course, so there would be obvious reasons for people coming and going. The back of the building would serve as their church. The sound of music might present a problem because of the closeness of homes.

The second possibility was an empty warehouse at the edge of the village – a much more spacious facility, but quite remote. Its location might not attract new members, but there would be less of a chance of being discovered. They had to decide which was more important – growth of their church or safety.

The third option was an entirely different concept: *a brand-new church built entirely with government funds, even built on a free piece of land*. All they had to do, they were told, was apply for a license and be "chosen." Jian explained how this could happen:

"I am a retired teacher. That profession, as you may know, required me to be atheist, which I agreed to when I entered the university. I remained an atheist for most of my working years, until my wife introduced me to Christianity shortly before my retirement. I eventually converted and joined her underground church. When it grew to the point of being too large for reasons of safety, my wife and I started our own house church. This was when I was no longer a teacher, of course. Our congregation grew to fifteen people, which was a lot for a house church. That was when we made the decision to merge with your church. Please do not misunderstand what I am about to tell you because my wife and I love this church. This is where we want to be...always! I am only passing this information on to you as I received it from a friend of mine who is still teaching and has to remain loyal to the requirements of his professional calling.

"Even though my friend and I do not usually discuss religion, he told me that a piece of land close to his home has been made available from the governor of our province for a Three Self Church. It is just outside our village to the north and waiting only for someone to apply for an official license. I do not know much about the Three Self Church except that it stands for self-governance, self-support, and self-propagation. It is sanctioned by our country's government and therefore rejects interference of any kind from foreign governments. It is supposedly a *different form of Christianity*.

"This is just another option that might be available to us. In all fairness to our staff and church, I felt I should put it on the table for discussion."

The Three Self Church option dominated their discussion for the next two hours. Nuo, who belonged to a Three Self Church for several years, was able to answer all their questions.

Roberto and Elena were also somewhat knowledgeable about this particular church as well as many of the other religions of China plus some philosophies such as Confucianism, but their knowledge was limited to articles, papers, books, and theological discussions. They listened intently as Nuo and each of their other staff members talked about their own personal backgrounds and what led them to the Christian Church. The testimonies were amazing – many different religions described in detail...the perceptions and the realities.

It was time for a momentous decision regarding the future of their church!

Appropriately, Jian was the first to speak once again regarding the Three Self Church option: "I think we have all been enlightened by Nuo about the benefits and drawbacks of the Three Self Church. While a brand-new church initially sounds exciting, especially with the expectation of government funds, I feel the benefits are dwarfed in comparison with the confinements. I am <u>not</u> in favor of giving up the freedoms we currently have in determining our own sermons and conducting Bible studies. Nor do I want to be part of a 'different form of Christianity' that, if I understand it correctly, is a distortion of the real gospel truth."

Everyone agreed. Option 3 was discarded.

Next to be eliminated was the building in the heart of the village. The issues of danger and music put aside, at the rate their church was already growing, it probably would not be large enough for very long.

The unanimous decision then was to keep their current Christian identity and opt for "safety over growth" by purchasing and renovating the empty warehouse at the edge of the village. If they kept everything quiet and unobtrusive, they hoped their local government would continue to ignore them. Tai and Jian agreed to work out the logistics, convene a second meeting for final approval, and handle the transaction.

Many hands made the transition easy. The building had been vacant for more than three years and the owner was happy to have it taken off his hands for a reasonable sum. The inside cleaned up nicely and held more benches than they originally estimated it would. Every member wanted to help. There were donations of Bibles, communion supplies, paper and pencils for children, music books and music stands. Those who could not help with material gifts made food for the workers. There was something for everyone to do; each member felt a part of their new church home.

They decided to keep the exterior exactly as it was, still looking like an old warehouse – no signs, no visible changes.

It was almost finished...a couple more walls to paint and some clean-up to do on the floors. They were days away from holding their first service.

Jian was standing on a tall ladder leaned up against a wall, patching a few small cracks near the ceiling, when the ground rumbled and shook! The top of the ladder slid sideways, almost to the point of tipping over. Roberto rushed to hold it steady while Jian scrambled down. The shaking continued.

"Everyone – get out of the building!" Roberto shouted as things that were on tables started falling to the floor.

They hurried outside, trying to keep their balance as they ran. People were pouring out of the houses and into the streets, running *toward them* – toward the edge of town! Others were confused, standing still, not knowing what to do or where to go. The sound of cracking walls added to the panic as people tried to escape falling debris.

Roberto pointed toward a field just past their church, pushing Elena in that direction. "Go there! Follow Elena! Hurry!"

Elena led the way, holding onto the hands of their two young children. Roberto was last, his arms supporting two elderly church members. They all sat huddled together in the field as the tremors became more intense, then stopped and started, stopped and started again, finally dying down.

Earthquakes were not uncommon. Everyone was used to the shaking that occurred regularly throughout the country, but this time it was different. It was more than the mild tremors usually felt in their village. This was an actual, full-blown earthquake. People were scared.

Roberto, Cheng, Tai, and Jian walked among their members gathered in the field. Is anyone missing, they asked? No; everyone was accounted for, but several were hurt.

They waited. Would there be more aftershocks? There were, but after a couple of hours, people started filtering back into the village to assess the damage.

The earthquake was strong, but not *totally* devastating. Their new church home stood! Some of the things that fell to the floor were broken and there were new wall cracks, but the structure itself proved hardy. Roberto, Elena, and some of the congregation began putting things back in order while others left, anxious to assess the damage to their homes.

Information started coming in from the village. Most of the older homes and buildings did not fare well – they were either severely damaged or destroyed beyond repair, including the building in the middle of the village that was one of the options for their new church! Members of the congregation who returned to their homes and found them destroyed began returning to church, bringing with them relatives, displaced friends and neighbors. Roberto and his staff decided their church was stable enough to provide temporary shelter for those who needed it.

The first outreach mission of their new church home became, of necessity, to house the homeless.

Other members of the congregation whose homes were still intact returned with blankets, food and medical supplies for their unexpected guests.

Cheng and Su-Li hurried home as well and breathed a sigh of relief when they got close and could see it standing. The damage appeared minimal from the outside. When they went inside, they were met by Qiang, a woman they did not know, and a young boy.

"Mother! Father! I am so glad you are alright! We didn't know where you were. This is Wu Liang and her son, Shing. They do not live far from me and I watched their building fall apart. As I ran to help them, my own apartment fell. Can Wu and Shing stay here?"

"Of course," replied Cheng. "Your friends are welcome, although we will be poor hosts for we cannot stay. We came back to see the extent of our home's damage and thankfully it does not look bad. We need to get extra blankets and food to take to our church for those who no longer have homes; there are so many."

"Thank you, Father. I am going back to my neighborhood to see what I can do to help, but first I want to look in on Mulan and make sure she is alright. She will be grateful to know Wu and Shing are staying here in safety."

"Mulan will be grateful?" As Su-Li's eyes met those of Wu, she suddenly realized that their guests were Guang's wife and son! "Please bring Mulan here also if she needs shelter," said Su-Li, much to Cheng's surprise. "Wu, we would be thankful if you could see to Mulan's comfort in our absence if Qiang brings her here."

"Yes, I will. Thank you. Shing and I will be pleased to take care of Mulan. Qiang, could we go with you in case you need help with her?"

"I should be able to do it alone, Wu. Right now, I think Shing needs to stay here where it is safe and get some rest. I will be back soon, either with Mulan or to let you know she is alright. Father, if you need anything, Wu will know where to find me." He blended into the crowded street.

After making sure their guests were made somewhat comfortable, Cheng and Su-Li gathered bedding and supplies and hurried back to the church.

###

Meanwhile, darkness was setting in; lamps were lit as their building continued to fill with people. Some had managed to salvage clothing, food, and cherished belongings which they brought with them; others had nothing. Many were injured; medical supplies were scarce.

Searching for missing family and friends went on through the night. Workers left and came back at a steady pace, bringing more hurt and displaced people as they were rescued from the rubble, staying only long enough themselves to eat, rest for a short time, and go back out.

"Roberto! We have no more room and there are still people coming in. Can we reopen our old mission house if it is safe?" asked Elena.

"Of course we can! Why didn't I think of it? I still have the key! If nothing else, we can at least give people a roof over their heads and a place to lie down. Give me time to make sure it's safe. If it isn't, I'll be back within an hour. If I'm not back by then, have our members start bringing people over. If Cheng and Su-Li come back by then, perhaps they can bring the first group and stay there with them. They know that building better than anyone."

Cheng and Su-Li arrived just minutes after Roberto's departure and received their assignment. When an hour had passed without Roberto's return, they picked up the bedding and supplies they just brought from home and, with the help of two other workers, carefully wound their way through littered streets, leading several dozen villagers to their old mission house. Roberto had the stove in the middle of the room fired up and was bringing in another load of wood – hopefully enough to keep it going for the rest of the night. Then he and the other two workers hurried back to the new church to assemble another group.

Cheng and Su-Li got busy making their weary guests as comfortable as possible with what little they had. Families huddled together. Parents were trying to get scared children to sleep amid the confusion and continuing aftershocks, finally falling asleep themselves through sheer exhaustion.

Clean up, recovery, and rescue started with fresh vigor at the first light of day, although it was well into the afternoon when new helpers arrived to allow Cheng and Su-Li time to rest for a few hours. When they arrived home, they were greeted from the sitting room with a wave from an injured but smiling Mulan.

"I was so relieved to hear Qiang's voice calling me!" she told them. "I stood in the doorway when the earthquake started, as we were always told to do, but the doorway came apart. I fell forward and a piece of heavy wood landed on top of me. It was across my back, holding me down. Qiang pulled me free, but my legs would not hold me up...so he carried me here. Wu has been doctoring me all night and Shing slept right here on the floor next to me. He wouldn't leave me either. Thank you, my friends, for welcoming my family and me into your home."

"Family." Su-Li had not thought about Mulan having family. Although Guang was gone, she was blessed with a caring daughter-in-law and grandson. "Our home is your home, Mulan, for as long as you and your family wish to stay," she heard Cheng say.

Noise from the streets did not bother Cheng or Su-Li at all as they finally collapsed onto their bed for much-needed sleep. They awoke to the delicious aroma of fresh cooking. Wu was sautéing vegetables she had retrieved from Mulan's garden.

With apologies for having so little time to eat or to spend with their guests, Cheng and Su-Li gathered extra cooking pots and medical supplies to take back to their old mission house. Wu gave them bread and more cooked vegetables to feed as many of the people in their care as possible. It wasn't a lot, but Cheng and Su-Li were thankful for whatever they had that they could share.

Mulan healed quickly. The numbness in her legs left and, with help from Qiang and Cheng, most of her home was soon restored to a habitable condition. Cheng and Su-Li could not help but notice

72

Mulan's joy as she was finally able to welcome her daughter-in-law and grandson into her home. People were too busy to notice, care, or ask questions. The village was still in chaos.

Repairing and rebuilding homes was a slow process, but every time one of the families in Roberto's church was able to go back home, it was a time of shared celebration. As soon as enough of the people were able to leave, he closed the old mission house once again and concentrated all efforts on re-repairing their new facility.

It was Saturday afternoon when Roberto called another staff meeting. "It is going to be a long time before all of our guests can return to their homes or find new ones," he said. "I feel we should go ahead with a worship service as normal tomorrow. Do you think we could do it in that corner if we move some of the supplies out of the way and straighten it up?"

Yes, they could! It would be close quarters, but they *wanted* to make it happen! Roberto and Yi Ze, their Chinese interpreter, announced that night that there was going to be a church service in the morning and everyone was invited who wished to attend.

Never had Su-Li felt so good about playing her music as she did that Sunday! Their church members were elated to hear the joyful music again. Many of their guests were wary at first, even though they were invited, still feeling that they should stay outside. But curiosity and the music pulled them in. Su-Li caught glimpses of people moving about, gradually coming closer, some even sitting on the floor in front of them as they played their traditional Chinese instruments and sang. It was like turning on a light in the darkness. Faces were changing from despair and sadness to smiles as the music drew attention away from their homeless plight. More people started coming in from outside. The church came to life as Roberto welcomed everyone with a message of love and a sense of community.

After the sermon, the musicians changed over to their western instruments and handed out Chinese/English song sheets. Su-Li's guitar playing had improved considerably in the months since her birthday. All the hours of practice and perseverance enabled her to strum along very naturally now as she played and sang with the others. She loved her new instrument of choice.

She knew that something they did that day made a difference. As weeks went by and more of their guests were able to return to their homes, many came back to visit, say thank you once again, and help others who were still there. Some joined the church and affirmed their new-found Christian faith. The congregation grew quicker than any of them could have anticipated. What Roberto and Elena and others kept hearing was that their church provided something that was lacking in people's lives...love! – brotherly, Christian love, and caring for others. They wanted to hear more about God, and how Jesus, the son of God, loved all the people of the world so much that he was willing to die an excruciating death to give them eternal life. They wanted to learn more about the Resurrection, Heaven...and hope. Their children delighted in the stories Nuo told about Noah's ark, Moses, and Jonah and the whale. They laughed heartily at the idea of a man being swallowed by a big fish and not being let out until he agreed to cooperate!

Once again, Roberto and Elena and their staff were faced with a situation of not enough room for their crowded congregation. It was a good problem to have, but one that needed to be resolved. They considered splitting their church into several smaller ones.

They prayed for guidance and for another door to open for them – specifically, a *safe* door.

Their prayers were answered by an unexpected person – Wu Liang. "I have a very large building on the other side of the village," she explained to Cheng and Su-Li, "near where I used to live. Guang and I were going to start a decorating business where we could offer my paintings and other pieces of art for sale. I took mostly art classes in school and have already sold many pieces that Guang took with him when he traveled to Beijing and other cities. The merchants always waited for Guang to return with more, buying whatever I sent with him."

When he traveled? Guang was just full of surprises, thought Su-Li. Whoever would have imagined Guang being a business person of any kind or even having a "real job" other than the one she used to hate. What kind of job *did* he have she wondered? Retail stores? Real estate?

"We intended to renovate," Wu continued, "so I would have a gallery for my finished work as well as a private studio where I could paint and create my models of pottery, metal, and wood. We knew there would still be a lot more space than we needed and were going to rent parts of it out to other businesses. But now...*but now* that cannot happen."

The "catch" in Wu's voice was not lost on Cheng or Su-Li. It spoke quietly of a lost love.

"With Qiang's help, I have found another place for my studio and gallery – a smaller place, not requiring as much work. It was partially damaged from the earthquake and the owner offered it to Qiang for a sum much less than he would have accepted if the building was in good condition or if he knew a woman was going to be the owner. We have been working on it for months and it is almost ready for me to move in. In return for all of Qiang's help, I am going to loan part of the building to him for creating his beautiful wooden instruments. His apartment is no longer big enough for him and his business."

Cheng and Su-Li both knew their son loved music and, like his mother, could play many instruments without ever having had a lesson. They also knew he was talented in working with wood. However, creating musical instruments was something Qiang had not shared with them. *Ah, my enterprising son,* Cheng mused with a quiet chuckle!

"Recently, when Qiang told me about the need of your church for more space," Wu continued, "I decided that I might be able to help. If my old building is suitable, and if your church will help me pay for my new small building, I will give you the larger one."

Roberto, Elena, and the rest of their staff could not believe their eyes when they inspected Wu's facility. It was twice the size of the building they were currently in and, yes, it would take some fixing, but it was perfect. Even the location was ideal – still on the outskirts of the village. By all appearances, it looked like an uninteresting, slightly damaged storage structure.

Cheng took care of all the financial transactions involved in selling their current "warehouse," paying off Wu's new smaller studio and gallery, obtaining ownership of the larger building for their church (officially listed as a produce processing market), and depositing a good sum of residual money with Roberto and Elena to cover restoration costs.

A few weeks later, Wu presented them with an experimental piece of her art work – a glass cross to hang over the inside door of their new church building – a *lighted* cross.

Electricity was coming to their village! The governor decided that because so many homes and buildings needed to be replaced after the earthquake, it was a good time to install the power lines for electricity that were now available for their province.

Wu was excited about the possibility of having power in her new studio and creating lighted or moving pieces of art.

Soon there could also be electricity in the more remote area outside their village – maybe in Roberto and Elena's church. If so, the first thing they intended to plug in was Wu's cross...a beacon of light that she silently offered in memory of her beloved Guang.

SHOES IN THE RIVER

Chapter 7: A Turn in the Road

1998 - 1999

Roberto and Elena did not have much time to enjoy their spacious new building. The first officially-called gathering of the congregation in their new facility was to say good-bye and introduce their replacements. It was time for them to return to their own country.

Su-Li remembered how she resisted meeting Roberto and Elena six years ago, thinking they could not possibly be as good at leading the church as their predecessors. How wrong she was. Now she hated the thought of saying good-bye to these special friends who were almost like family.

She recalled how they helped her cope with the grief she kept clinging to over the loss of her children, finally making it possible for her to move on. And when Guang died and Qiang left home to take his place, there were no questions – just support for Cheng and Su-Li under an umbrella of genuine Christian love. *But how much did they really know,* Su-Li wondered? *Were they aware of Qiang's true mission? Did they know about the cave? Were others in their church involved?* She would never know the answers to any of these questions as neither Roberto nor Elena ever discussed the personal issues of any of their congregation with others.

Now it was time to stand in line to offer hugs and well wishes to these *spiritual* friends, knowing their *physical* paths would probably never cross again.

"Life goes on, even as the world changes. We also must be willing to change."

She would never forget those parting words from Roberto. There certainly *had been* a lot of changes in all their lives since he and Elena arrived! Together, they worked hard, grew the church, and studied the gospel. She didn't want them to leave, but it was time.

Cheng and Su-Li continued down the line to welcome Harry and Evelyn and 7-year-old Kate.

From the puzzled looks on everyone's faces, it was obviously going to take a while for the congregation to get used to Harry and Evelyn's "strange" English. How could the same language sound so different coming from the three English-speaking countries of their missionary families? The only one who seemingly had no problem understanding them was Cheng, undoubtedly because of his company's international contacts.

"I know it sometimes sounds like they are not finished talking yet," Cheng said to an exasperated Su-Li, "but you will understand them in time, probably sooner than you think, after your ears get used to the way their voices rise and fall. I know it is different from the way we learned English, but just listen to the "eh?" at the end of a sentence. Then you know they are finished talking and are waiting for you to respond or agree. Perhaps we are all going to get an education in international communications!"

His teasing continued as he added... "or maybe we will all be talking like them in a few years. Do you think I should offer a course to our members on how to understand and speak the 'new' English?"

Actually, it sounded like a pretty good idea to Su-Li! Then maybe she wouldn't feel so foolish when one of them said something and was obviously waiting for an answer to a question that she didn't understand.

But it wasn't just the accent that confused her – it was the strange new words! Earlier in the day Harry was talking about having a problem with something under the bonnet of his car. She couldn't imagine where there would be a hat in an automobile – or a boot. And Evelyn was talking about not being able to sit on her chesterfield because there was a tea spill on it and she had to wait for it to dry. It was obviously some kind of a seat. Cheng was right...she would just have to listen closer and not be afraid to ask questions!

Another thought was: If she and the other members of their congregation were having a hard time figuring out what their new church leaders were saying, maybe it wasn't one-sided. Maybe they were looking at this communications glitch from just their own perspective. Were Harry and Evelyn having difficulty as well? What about little Kate? Was she confused? Did they take language lessons before they came to China? If not, they might also need help.

Su-Li decided to tutor their new missionary family. She would talk to them after the service next Sunday and extend an offer of "mutual understanding!"

###

It was Tuesday morning. Cheng was packing for a trip to the port of Tianjin to inspect a cargo shipment scheduled to be off-loaded Thursday, then returning home on Friday or Saturday. He did not particularly care for traveling, but his job as Account Manager occasionally required him to also be an inspector and verify the accuracy of goods being received by his firm. He was told last week that there was a considerable discrepancy in what was ordered from a company in Mexico and what their copy of the bill of lading showed as being delivered. Cheng and two of his peers from the Tianjin Operations Department, Huan and Yao, were instructed to be on site at the dock Thursday morning and physically open and inspect two of the containers before making a decision whether to allow the rest of the shipment to be off-loaded and transported over land to Beijing. It could take just a couple of hours or it could take days.

In the past, Cheng never minded these short trips for his company if Su-Li went with him. It was an opportunity to combine business and pleasure by spending good quality time together, enjoying some different scenery, and returning home at their leisure.

But she wasn't going to accompany him on this trip. Instead, she was going to help Wu move into her new studio, and was looking forward to seeing some of her art work. Qiang's studio was going to be in the same building and she wanted to see what it looked like, anticipating it might need a little "dressing up."

"One last chance, Pu," Cheng called out from the bedroom. "Are you sure you don't want to change your mind and come with me? I can wait for you to pack. There's plenty of time."

For a fleeting moment, Su-Li had second thoughts. Maybe she should go with Cheng. She knew his dislike for traveling alone and it always *was* refreshing to get away from her usual routine for a few days. But Wu graciously gave up her big building for the good of their church and Su-Li did not feel she should back out of the offer she made to help her get set up – nor did she want to. In a strange way, she felt consoled by having an opportunity to help Guang's family...almost like a silent apology for the way she treated him. Besides, she truly liked Wu from the first time they met during the earthquake. No, this is where she needed to be.

"You know how much I enjoy being with you, my dear, sweet husband," – and she paused long enough to give him her own smile as he poked his head around the corner in anticipation... "but I am needed here."

So, without Su-Li's company, Cheng just wanted to get there, get the job done, and get home! Suitcase, briefcase and jacket in hand, he kissed her goodbye, ambled out to his ten-year-old but still reliable 1988 Volkswagen® company car, and drove to Tianjin.

###

The dock area was crowded with workers, crewmen, and containers as Cheng and Huan wound their way through the maze toward their destination. The other company associate, Yao, was held up in traffic, so Cheng and Huan decided to go ahead without him and locate the containers in question. Hopefully by then Yao would be there and they could proceed with their inspection.

While Huan boarded the ship to find the captain, Cheng waited on the dock for Yao, shuffling through a handful of papers. He reviewed the list of circled items that were supposedly included in the shipment but not ordered by his company. Perhaps they were mislabeled...or perhaps they were just plain wrong. Whatever the problem, Cheng hoped it would be easy to resolve so he could get back to the hotel and prepare for an early morning departure.

His beeper was buzzing; he looked up at the deck of the ship where Huan was waving for him to come aboard. He tucked the papers back into his briefcase and headed up the gangplank. Huan and the captain found the two containers which luckily were on the top tier.

"Are these the only two we need to check out?" Huan asked as he pointed to the two containers.

Cheng confirmed the container numbers with his list. "Probably. If these two are alright, the others should be also. Is there room up here to open them?"

"No. The captain said it would take too long and we would be in the way for offloading other cargo. He wants them taken down to the dock. Should I tell him we are agreeable?"

"Certainly," said Cheng. You talk with the captain while I go back down and find a crane operator and reserve some dock space."

Yao was waiting below when Cheng returned, apologetic for being late, knowing it was frowned upon by their company. "You haven't missed much," Cheng reassured him. "We've located the two containers and we're going to bring them down. Huan is going to stay on deck while they're lifted. How about looking for a crane operator while I find someone to approve the dock space. I want to put them down right over here if we can. I'm thinking this whole thing is clerical error and not product error because it looks like everything in question on these pages, which is all the stuff in the first container, is consistently one line-item description off from what we ordered."

"I hope you're right, Cheng. Maybe somebody just had a bad day. Hold on - I think that's the guy I need to talk to over there. I'll be right back."

Twenty minutes later, the first container was secured. Cheng and Yao moved to the side of the dock as the giant crane lifted the container up and off the ship and over the water, moving it gracefully through the air until it was almost directly over its approved dock space.

SNAP!

Cheng and Yao looked up in surprise and froze as they watched a frayed metal cable slicing through the air above them and the now-tilted railway container following close behind on a clumsy arc path as it pulled loose from a second and third tether seconds before crashing to the concrete dock. Cheng and Yao had no time to take a step in any direction as its shadow covered them. They stood helplessly as it fell from the sky and snuffed out their lives.

Su-Li sensed something was wrong when the two strangers came to her door late in the evening, identifying themselves as friends of Cheng, and asking if they might come in. Her voice trembled as she moved aside for them to enter and asked the obvious question:

"Is something wrong? Where is Cheng?"

They motioned for her to sit down and then sat down across from her before answering. An icy coldness gripped her as unbelievable words spilled from the mouth of one of the strangers:

"I am Li Ju and this is Tai Ying. We are both friends of your husband. We are sorry to bring you sad news from our company...and there is no easy way to say this. There was an accident on one of the docks in Tianjin today when a container that was being off-loaded broke from its cables. Cheng and another man were killed; they died instantly."

This could not be true! She buried her face in her hands, **knowing** that when she opened her eyes and looked up, there would be no one there. This would just be a dream and she would wake up. But the thought of looking up and seeing the two men still there terrified her. Then it would be real. She felt a hand on her arm as one of the men moved over next to her. She looked up into kind eyes.

"I am so sorry, Su-Li. We were all shocked to learn of this tragedy. Tai and I asked if we could be the ones to come here tonight as we were Cheng's personal friends at work. We felt that he would have wanted it this way, rather than an official representative of the company calling on you."

Numbness. Shock. Disbelief. As the world started swirling around her, she had a moment of lucidness, or maybe it was denial. Yes, she remembered Cheng talking about Li and Tai several times. They were his friends and, right now, they were her guests! She stood, straightened her posture, and with as much composure as she could muster, tried to regain enough presence of mind to be a polite hostess.

"May I pour you some tea?" she asked hoarsely.

She hardly heard her own words as she tried to speak above the strange buzzing noise in her head – like the rising sound of a swarm of locusts.

Why were they staring at her like that? Why didn't they answer? Her hands suddenly felt clammy and her throat wanted to close. She tried to take a step but her legs felt like they belonged to someone else. Her fall was broken by the arms of the two visitors who were instantly at her side.

She had never fainted before! It was a strange, out-of-control sensation, and she was embarrassed, but it soon passed.

"Where can we find Qiang?" asked Li.

She recited his address.

"I am going to go to his apartment now. Tai is going to stay with you until I return with Qiang. If I cannot locate him, is there someone else I can contact? We are not going to leave you alone."

"Yes. My friend, Mulan, lives only a short distance from here. Please ask her to come even if you find Qiang."

Li wrote down both addresses and disappeared into the night. Tai sat next to her, placing a shawl and comforting arm around her shoulders while she shivered uncontrollably. Mulan's voice was a welcome sound as she rushed into the house. A few deep breaths, a soft handkerchief, and a cup of hot tea brought her back to the overwhelming reality of the night.

Qiang arrived, blinking back tears as he reached down and hugged his mother. It was the longest hug she had ever received from her son. The two men offered condolences again and left.

"Li and Tai will be back in a couple of days, Mother," Qiang told her. "They said they will have some papers for us to sign and will go over all the company business with us. I thanked them for their kindness and for letting us have time to rest and think."

The days that followed were a blur; nothing seemed real. Qiang took care of the paperwork. Su-Li signed wherever Qiang placed an "X," not really knowing or caring what it was for. Mulan's presence was comforting; she did everything that needed to be done to prepare Su-Li's home for receiving friends after the funeral.

Harry and Evelyn, as new as they were, became instant care-givers. It even brought somewhat of a smile to Su-Li's face when Evelyn told her that the entire congregation of their church would have descended on her home with food, love, and support if they could have, but Harry told them to bide their time. There would be opportunities for all of that later. Right now, Su-Li needed peace and only limited visits while she prepared for Cheng's service.

Neighbors and friends made everything orderly. Cheng would have been pleased with all of their help, she thought, and just as equally for the assistance from his friends Li and Tai. She felt totally surrounded by kindness and friendship...but at the same time, so alone!

Why? she asked herself again and again. *Why didn't I go with Cheng on his trip? He wanted me to go with him. Why was it more important to help others than to be with my husband? Wu and Qiang would have gotten moved in and set up without me. I know I could not have changed what happened, but at least I would have been there!*

Her heart ached every time the reality of Cheng being gone touched it. She missed him desperately. There were so many things on her mind...so many thoughts; so many worries!

Qiang. Undoubtedly, he was going to be by her side through this whole thing, but how were people going to treat him? She knew the stigma attached to him as the "child executioner." Did Harry and Evelyn know? There was still the perception that he was sent away from their home in disgrace. Would people despise him? Tolerate him? Ignore him? She couldn't stand the thought of people unleashing anger against her son.

Mulan. Would her mere presence give rise to suspicions of their friendship? Had anyone noticed Mulan coming to her house to help? Would she still be rejected? She was just now starting to feel somewhat accepted again by people in the village. Would her presence ignite old animosity? The thought of her friend Mulan having to deal with old hatred stung her heart as well.

Wu. Guang's wife could blend into the crowd as she was not known, but what would happen if Shing clung to Mulan's side as a child would to a grandparent? Would Wu's and Shing's identities be discovered?

She had so many questions; so many worries, and no one to talk to...*at least no one she could see.* She prayed constantly to God, hoping He would hear her. She talked to Cheng every night before she went to bed, hoping that *somehow* he could hear. She searched her own mind for answers. Nothing. It was like waiting for an explosion to happen and not being able to do anything about it, with only the wind to listen to her fears.

She felt imminent doom and there was no one to hang onto, no one to understand.

It was the day before the "celebration of Cheng's life," as her church preferred the funeral to be called. Evelyn arrived mid-morning to go over final preparations. Su-Li sat quietly as Evelyn laid out the details, gently asking a few more questions about what she wanted to do after the service.

That was when Su-Li's world crashed. Composure was gone; humanness bared; and her overwhelming grief finally erupted and spilled over. Evelyn somehow knew it was coming and was prepared with tissues. She let her cry, patiently sitting next to her with a comforting arm over her shoulders.

"I am so sorry, Evelyn. *Thinking* about everything is easier than talking about it out loud. I am alright now. I won't go to pieces again – I promise. There are just a lot of things on my mind."

"I know there are, Su-Li, and you have been unbelievably strong. But you don't have to apologize for being human, and you don't have to be strong alone, eh?"

"Eh" made her smile as she remembered Cheng joking about the English ending sentences with "eh?" Although Evelyn's words were comforting, they didn't calm the troubling issues she would be faced with tomorrow. Cheng was the only person she ever confided in since they were married. Her parents were not far away physically, but were distant personally. According to tradition, she was now considered part of Cheng's family, not that of her birth parents. She was somewhat close to her sister and her two brothers and their families, but they were all busy with their own lives. Cheng's parents lived hundreds of kilometers away; she only saw them once a year. They knew nothing of their situation with Qiang.

Although Evelyn was a nice person, she was too new and too "different" to help...*or so she thought!*

Su-Li was stunned at what Evelyn said next and so openly. She put the tissues and teacups aside, looked directly into Su-Li's face: "I know all about what your family has been through, Su-Li. I know about the loss of your children, your grief over many years, your son's involvement in the cause for saving the babies of this village, and the burden that he carries. I know about everything you and Cheng have done for the growth of the church that Harry and I are privileged to be a part of. I know about the special friendship you have with Mulan and her daughter-in-law and grandson. I dared not speak to you about any of these things until now – until I knew for sure that you needed me.

"Now let's talk about how we are going to deal with all the worries that are on your mind and on your heart!"

Su-Li sat straight up in her chair. She had to consciously close her mouth which had gaped open in surprise.

"I suppose to begin with you would like to know how I acquired all this information, eh?"

"Yes...yes I would. The loss of my children and my grief are well known, but how do you know about Qiang and Mulan and..."

"First of all, Su-Li," Evelyn interrupted, "let me tell you that I have been told these things in complete confidence and have not shared anything with anyone, not even Harry. Qiang himself came to me out of concern for you and your health. He felt you needed someone other than him to talk to now that Cheng was gone. He decided that Mulan could not be that person as you try to not be seen together. Wu could not be that person for fear that people might discover she was Guang's wife and think such a friendship with you would not be normal.

"After much prayer, I am told, Qiang decided he had to trust *someone* and he focused on the church and chose me. I feel honored to be entrusted with such knowledge. I know the consequences of this information being shared with anyone for any reason. I promise you that whatever we talk about today will remain within these walls."

It was like a curtain being drawn back from a covered window and a bright, beautiful light on the other side. Evelyn efficiently summed up everything needing to be done. All of Su-Li's concerns were addressed, thanks to her son and her new best friend.

"Now let's go over the details one more time," Evelyn said as she checked the items on her note paper. "As you requested, it will be a Christian service. You and Qiang will have your own private time in prayer before receiving friends.

"Qiang will stay by your side as people come through a line to offer condolences. As Cheng's only living child, that is where he felt he should be, even with the perception of his being sent away in disdain by you and Cheng. He will look into no one's eyes and will speak only if spoken to. Do not be concerned for Qiang; he will endure whatever coldness is directed at him.

"You and I agree then," Evelyn continued, "that you will speak to Mulan and explain to her that in her own best interest and for the sake of the cause of the children, she should come by and pay her respects to you and Qiang, but not stay. She should make an appearance and then quietly leave. You will also recommend to her that Wu should do the same, and not bring Shing with her as he knows you and Qiang and Mulan and it would be risky. Children will be children and you never know what they will say or do."

There. Everything Su-Li was worrying about was resolved and all the arrangements were in order. They spent the rest of the morning just "chatting" (Evelyn's word for "non-serious talking") and enjoying each other's company. It was peaceful.

Oddly enough, as they chatted, Su-Li realized that Evelyn's English was starting to make sense, just as Cheng predicted it would. All she had to do was *listen*, then if she didn't understand, ask questions...and she did! A boot turned out to be the trunk of a car; a bonnet was the hood; a chesterfield was a sofa. Chips were potatoes; gammon steak was ham. A spot of tea was the same as a cup of tea, and a cozy was a lovely quilted cover placed over a squatty looking teapot that kept it warm. Crumpets were little cakes served with a spot of tea. It was like learning another language.

"Oh, and one more thing," Evelyn said as she was preparing to leave: "If by happenchance (happenchance? *There* was another new word!) you are internalizing any blame for what befell Cheng and thinking something might have been different if you were with him, you need to do away with such thoughts. God's timing is perfect. When He decides to call us home to Heaven, we will go, not a moment sooner or later. It will not make any difference as to what our personal plans are. I can assure you that Cheng is with God because of God's will, and it will be the same with you and me and everyone else. All we can do when we have to let go of people we love is to be thankful for the time we had with them here on earth and know that *we will be together again.* Now please get some rest. I'll see you tomorrow morning, eh?"

Yes, she did know that, thanks to Roberto. His first sermon at their church six years ago spoke about "hope" and the promise of Heaven where she would be reunited with her lost children. She consoled herself knowing she would see Syaran and Xiu-Su again someday and they will all know each other. Cheng's absence was so fresh in her heart that she hadn't yet settled on the thought of seeing him again someday. Yes! They will be together again...in Heaven!

She silently thanked God for Evelyn and her church family; for Qiang, her precious son who was still here in this world looking after her; and for the years she and Cheng had shared. She slept better that night, wrapped in the knowledge that God was in charge of her life so she didn't have to be.

Qiang stood quietly at her side, speaking only to those who spoke to him, although Su-Li did notice several people turning around and leaving when they saw him. It was better to leave, she thought, than to treat him poorly. *Someday,* she told herself, *they will know the truth and appreciate Qiang for the good person he is, just as I have come to appreciate Guang. Yes, someday, they will know.*

The celebration of Cheng's life was a beautiful service that elicited memories, smiles, and tears. Su-Li had her own sad and happy moments, recalling special times with her husband of twenty-four years. She tried to keep her thinking positive, *knowing* that she will see him again.

Adjusting to life without Cheng was lonely and difficult, even though she still talked to him every night, asking his opinion on decisions that had to be made. Then she prayed to God, the *real* decision maker. Somehow the answers always became apparent – well, all except for one that she initially agonized over: what to do with Cheng's car. His company donated it to Su-Li for her family's use. A car was valuable, even an old one, as not every family could afford such a luxury. But Qiang didn't need it – he had one of his own that was newer. So, not seeing any clear path laid out before her, she made the decision on her own to keep it and learn to drive. If she was going to visit any of their family in the future, she needed a way to get there. Besides, driving didn't look particularly difficult – she watched Cheng drive for years and was pretty sure she could do everything just like he did. She signed up for driving lessons.

It was slow going...*very* slow. Cars and even bicycles were going around her as she concentrated on not getting too close to the edge of the road or taking more than her share of the middle. She finally agreed with the instructor that sitting higher on a pillow or cushion might help her see the road better. He was right – it did make a difference! After weeks of lessons and two good test drives with the instructor, she was feeling pretty comfortable behind the wheel, ready to make her first solo trip. She decided to drive to the other side of the village and see how Wu's gallery looked since it got decorated...plus look in on Qiang's quarters.

She also wanted Qiang's advice on a strange thumping sound coming from somewhere under the bonnet of her car.

"I think the thumping noise is a piston or a rod, Mother. You should probably think about trading this beauty in for a newer model, preferably before it leaves you stranded somewhere. Your other choice is to spend quite a bit of money to get this one repaired. But remember, it is eleven years old and has very high mileage. It would probably be wise to consider a newer car."

Su-Li agreed. She remembered Cheng talking about getting a newer model car for quite a while but hated to let this one go because it was running well. Even though it was a company car, his financial background caused him to be conservative. She could still hear his words of caution: "Take good care of what you have. Don't spend money on another car if the one you have is working fine and not costing much for repairs. Then buy a used one, as a new car loses its value quickly."

Well, that is what she would do, she decided...buy a new used car. "Where can I find a newer car, Qiang?"

"Let me look around and see what is available. For now, though, you might not want to drive this one any more than you absolutely have to."

Even though she was anxious to drive more, it wasn't terribly important to Su-Li. A lot of people in her village rode bicycles or walked, just like she always did when Cheng was working. Her bicycle was in excellent condition.

A week later Qiang brought information on a three-year old Volkswagen 1996 model that was for sale just a few kilometers away. He looked it over and decided it was a good reliable car.

"Want to take a look at it, Mother?"

She sure did, and what a difference from Cheng's 1988 model. This one had many more interesting gadgets and features than her old car, plus it was red...her favorite color!

"It needs new tires and you should probably take it in for an oil change before you go too far," Qiang recommended, "but other-wise, it's a good solid car and should do well for you. I would suggest you have the Volkswagen dealer do whatever work needs to be done."

The deal was sealed. Her new car was slightly smaller than Cheng's old one – a better size for her. She made an appointment with the dealer and drove her car in for service. To her delight, she was offered the comfort of a customer lounge while her car was getting new tires and a tune up.

A whole different world opened up for Su-Li. She loved driving and the independence of deciding where the road would take her. If her new car was as dependable as Cheng's old one, she was looking forward to many miles of road ahead and years of enjoyable driving!

In the meantime, however, there was still more business to wrap up. Cheng was not only a good business financial person, she was told by his company's personnel representative, he was a good provider for his family. He had an insurance policy and numerous funds put aside for his retirement; now it was up to her to decide how the funds should be allocated. When she first looked at the array of computer forms spread out on the table in front of her, she regretted dropping out of that accounting class in college so she could add another music study to her curriculum.

All she had to do was "follow the (complicated and tedious) instructions, read descriptions, make choices, check the appropriate boxes with an X, and the computer would do the rest."

Once again Qiang offered good advice. "Why don't we talk with Huan, Mother? He took over Father's responsibilities in the accounting department and probably knew Father better than anyone. He left his card for us after the funeral and said he would be glad to help in any way he could."

Consulting with Huan proved to be a good decision. As the three of them sat around a table, Huan explained the options and made good recommendations for disbursements over the long term – good solid choices, nothing risky. "Cheng invested wisely," Huan explained. "The growth was slow but steady; the funds in his accounts should allow you to live as comfortably as you do now...as long as you don't get carried away with big expensive sports cars," he added with a smile.

For a brief, painful moment, he reminded her of Cheng and how he used to kid her and then flash a handsome grin. "If I ever feel the urge to trade in my Volkswagen for a big expensive sports car, I will call you first so you can talk me out of it!" she replied with her own humor.

Chapter 8: School

1999 - 2000

It was a relief for Su-Li to know she did not have to depend on anyone to support her, even for a short time. When she graduated from the university twenty-six years ago with a music major and a minor in economics, she knew she could always get a job if she wanted to or needed to, but she never did. Now she wondered what it would take to bring her up to date as a music teacher in today's world. Maybe she should look into it...just in case something changes. Or perhaps she should brush up on economics and think about entering the business world. Either way, she would have to go back to school and take courses. She decided to visit Evelyn and ask her to pray with her for guidance. Silently she hoped music would be the answer rather than business. She loved the way music always seemed to bring joy to others. She wasn't sure that anything about business could bring joy.

"Good for you!" was Evelyn's enthusiastic reply. "I'm definitely in favor of women being able to support themselves, even if they don't have to. You are such a good musician, Su-Li, and so patient with young people; you would be a wonderful teacher. We have several university students in our church who might be able to steer you in the right direction, eh? At least they might be able to come up with a name or two to contact for information."

Weeks later, and armed with her carefully prepared portfolio, Su-Li drove to Beijing for an appointment with the university counselor.

"Your portfolio is impressive, Su-Li. You indicate here that you are currently playing several instruments on a regular basis, so your musical skills are probably not going to need updating. It would be to your advantage, however, to learn how to play a piano as well. Piano acumen with basic hands-on ability has emerged as the 'must have' for every teacher of music today. Would you be willing to learn? Do you have access to one?"

Yes, she would definitely be willing to learn! And yes, she did have access to one! About a year ago, her church acquired a piano from one of the families who stayed there after the earthquake. It was old and suffered damage from the tremors. It was covered with fallen roof debris. One corner was severely damaged and dirt got inside, but Qiang decided it was salvageable. He somehow made it look and sound relatively good again, much to Harry and Evelyn's delight. Even though it wasn't beautiful, it wasn't ugly either, and it would be perfectly fine for her to practice on, she decided.

The other courses she would have to take were refreshers to bring her up to the new curriculum level requirements. She piled the books in her car and headed home, eagerly looking forward to her exciting new challenge.

She studied with enthusiasm, consulting occasionally with the university students at her church. She was surprised at how much she remembered...and how much she had forgotten. But learning and relearning felt good!

Her biggest challenge, although a delightful one, was the piano. She played music mostly by ear, but *did* know how to read music, which made key location easy. The difficulty was coordinating four things at once – playing with two hands going in separate directions, mastering the pedals, and keeping her eyes on the music. But just like struggling to master her guitar, it was a matter of determination, lots of practice, and a love of creating music. She had no one to teach her the guitar, but she *did have* a willing piano teacher at church. She and Kang, one of the university students, spent many hours together each week *teaching and learning*. Su-Li taught Kang how to play the pipa and Kang gave Su-Li piano lessons.

Kang reinforced the guidelines set out by the university counselor: "It is not necessary to be able to play the piano like an accomplished musician, Su-Li, but rather to achieve a level where you can effectively teach others how to play by showing them the basics and putting them on the correct path to learning."

That was Su-Li's goal. She didn't expect to fall in love with playing the piano *herself*...but she did!

The two days of testing arrived. Su-Li drove to Beijing the day before, checked into a hotel near the campus, and nervously awaited the exams. Those day-before-the-exam jitters still gnawed at her stomach the same way they did twenty-six years ago!

But the nervousness she felt before the exams was mild compared to how she felt after the exams - two weeks later as she anxiously opened a letter from the university.

"We are pleased to inform you...," it began. Yes! She passed all the exams and was officially qualified to teach a music class! She was surprised and excited to receive a second letter weeks later, informing her of an opening for a music teacher at an elementary school in a neighboring village. She made an appointment for an interview...and was hired.

Su-Li could not believe how everything had fallen into place for her to be certified and offered a job so quickly. ***She was now a working woman!***

Her students were ages 6 through 11 and very excited about singing, dancing, and playing instruments. They were so full of energy and enthusiasm, and their eagerness to learn warmed her very soul. She had visions of her entire class putting on a performance by the end of the school year...until the first day on her new job when she saw the instruments.

They were pitiful. She learned that the school's music program was discontinued ten years earlier and the instruments piled on shelves in a furnace storage room. They were dirty, scratched, broken and rusting. The piano was not playable. The wires were dried and brittle; the keys discolored, chipped and warped. The top was cracked. One leg was splintered on the bottom, making it shorter than the other. She doubted that even Qiang, with all of his musical instrument expertise, could resurrect it.

"It will definitely be a challenge," he said with a whistle and a head scratch, "but not impossible. Despite what you see, the wood is solid, but I would have to get it to my shop somehow where I could work on it. It is going to take a lot of time and I wouldn't want to waste valuable hours driving back and forth when I could actually be working on it. I'm just not sure how to get it moved."

"Let me talk to Professor Zi, Qiang. As school administrator, I will first have to get his permission to have it restored. If he agrees, then we can decide how to move it; perhaps he will have some ideas. Meanwhile, do you think you can breathe life into some of these other instruments?"

"Well, they're going to be a lot easier than the piano. Let me take a couple with me and see what I can do while you're negotiating with the administrator on how to move this dinosaur."

Hua Zi looked at Su-Li as though she had lost her mind! "We were planning to cut that old piano up and throw it away as soon as we could afford a new one, but we have not been granted money in our budget for a piano. Are you telling me it can be restored?"

"I don't know, Professor Zi, but my son is willing to try at no cost to the school if we can get it to his studio. My own opinion is that if we can get it to sound right, regardless of how it looks, it would be good enough for children to learn on and worth the effort to move it, but it will be as you wish, of course."

"It will get moved."

In addition to being the school administrator, Hua Zi was a respected elder in the village. He knew everyone and "had ways of getting things done," not only in that village, but in many neighboring villages as well. Two days later, an army truck pulled up in front of the school with a ramp and a half-dozen soldiers. The out-of-kilter piano limped aboard, headed for Qiang's studio twenty-five kilometers away.

The restoration took months and an enormous amount of determination, but Qiang decided if his mother was willing to learn how to play a piano so she could teach children, he was willing to do whatever it took to bring this antique back to life for her. While he waited for new wires to arrive, he salvaged keys, pedals, and inner pieces from several scrapped pianos. He rebuilt and replaced damaged exterior wood and worked with the rest of the alligatored wood that was still in decent condition, patching, refinishing, and polishing. A final tuning, and it was finally time to call in his mother and the army and have it returned to school!

Hua Zi stared in amazement when Qiang uncovered the piano and the soldiers carefully rolled it down the ramp and into the school. It sat in the middle of the room like a proud relic – sitting level, cleaned, polished, broken keys and pedals replaced...and it worked beautifully! It still bore numerous scars from years of neglect, but the sound was rich and deep. Su-Li's students were so excited they could hardly sit still, all anxious to learn to play.

"Thank you, Qiang," said Hua Zi. "You are indeed as talented an artist as your mother is a musician and teacher. We are indebted to both of you."

Su-Li beamed. It felt good to hear kind words spoken to her son!

Kang, the pianist at Su-Li's church, saw the resurrected piano before it was transported back to Su-Li's school, and was just as impressed with the final result as Professor Zi. She shared Su-Li's enthusiasm to reinstate the love of music in the small country school, doing what she could to help. Knowing that Su-Li was still new at being a pianist herself, Kang gave her copies of easy-to-play children's songs – ones that her students could sing along with as they marched or danced around the room. Some were in Chinese, others in English and Spanish; many crossing over from one language to another like "Khua, Khua, Khua Mai Cheo" (Row, Row, Row Your Boat). One of their favorites was a nonsense song: "Mares Eat Oats and Does Eat Oats and Little Lambs Eat Ivy." When they speeded it up, it sounded more like "Mairzy doats and dozy doats, and liddle lamzy divey," in any language! It made them laugh, no matter how many times they sang it.

The other instruments...the ones that held any promise of rebirth, were taken home one or two at a time and worked on collectively by Su-Li, Qiang, and several musical friends. Every time an instrument was brought back to life, it was cause for celebration for the workers and the children.

But no one was happier than Su-Li. What a delight she felt when she saw the happy faces of her students as they tried each new arrival! She helped them appreciate the uniqueness of each instrument and its beautiful sounds. They brought such enjoyment. She just wished she had more of them. And with that thought, another idea was forming - but she would need Professor Zi's help again!

Professor Zi didn't say yes or no, only that he would think about it.

They worked hard to prepare for their first program. The children were dressed in their best clothes and adorned with brightly colored scarves and ribbons. The piano was rolled next to the window so it could be heard from outside, to be played by Kang, the pianist from Su-Li's church. Teachers, parents, other students, and villagers filled the schoolyard as the children proudly marched from the building, carrying their musical instruments and singing about a magic dragon called Puff while getting themselves lined up on risers in front of the audience.

Hua Zi smiled as he sat off to the side, watching parents wave to their children, pointing them out to others, and grinning like...well, like proud parents! Or maybe he was smiling at his own granddaughter as she marched by.

Su-Li was so proud of her class as they sang, danced, and took turns playing their sparse assortment of musical instruments. Their energy and enthusiasm were contagious. When they finished their performance and took a final bow, the audience stood, clapped and cheered. Such a warm, standing ovation called for an encore, and *it just so happened* that Su-Li and the children had one ready! It was a delightful experience for a school where music had not been part of the curriculum for so many years.

At the end of the program, Hua Zi took center stage. He personally thanked Su-Li, the students, and assistants for such an enjoyable program, then turned again to face the students.

"Hold up your musical instruments," he instructed.

Until now, Hua wasn't sure if he would follow through on the "subtle" suggestion Su-Li offered earlier, but after seeing the enthusiasm of the children and the audience, there was no hesitation. "As you can see," he began, "our school owns very few instruments and they are being shared by many students. We have not had a music teacher for many years, but now we are fortunate to not only have a good teacher, but one who has personally taken the time, along with the help of her son, to beautifully restore all of the instruments you see here, including the piano."

He paused for a few seconds to enjoy the murmurs of appreciation from the audience. "But this is all we have. Regretfully, we had to throw away many instruments because they were old and beyond repair. So, I would like to invite you to be a special part of our new music program and consider my request. If you happen to have any musical instruments at home that you no longer play or have use for, Teacher Ming will happily accept them in any condition. She is totally devoted to her mission of teaching music to our children, and I would encourage you to support her however you can."

He turned to Su-Li and smiled at her with an extended hand of appreciation as she gave a traditional polite nod to the clapping audience. Within a month, they had eighteen more instruments. Some were in excellent condition and others needed work, but it didn't matter - it was an ongoing labor of love. As her music class grew in size, activity, and musical ability, it gave birth to yet another possibility.

Wouldn't it be fun and educational, she thought, *to take my students...or at least some of them, to other schools to perform?* It was just an idea, but a persistent one.

###

It was also a time of *personal* growth for Su-Li. As she immersed herself in the world of music appreciation, Kang loaned her instruction books on correct fingering techniques and finer methods of playing piano. Su-Li spent countless hours practicing every week at school and church, challenging herself to play more and more difficult pieces. She delved deeper into the lives of classical music composers and artists. It became the new passion in her life.

Chapter 9: Dangerous Winds of Change

2000-2003

It was a time of relative peace in Su-Li's personal world, in spite of growing uneasiness around her. There were changes...and though she sensed them, resisted being pulled out of the small, comfortable space she had carved into her life and claimed as her own.

She was happy now. The emptiness she felt after Cheng died was slowly being filled with a stream of new activity and people – other teachers, precious students and their parents, musicians, church family, and Qiang's soon-to-be bride, Guo.

Guo was the granddaughter of the couple who owned the safe house where Qiang delivered newborn babies. She was in her second year at Peking University when she and Qiang met at her home – the second safe house, located just north of Beijing. They were casual acquaintances at first through their mutual mission, then became good friends, occasionally dating, then best friends, eventually realizing they were in love and wanting to spend the rest of their lives together. Qiang adhered to the same ingrained beliefs of his father – that love for a wife and family should be forever, true, and unconditional. Guo was the person he wanted to make that commitment to.

Su-Li could see and almost feel the total commitment Qiang and Guo had for each other. It was Guo who convinced Qiang to go back to school and finish his education, for which Su-Li was personally thankful.

Qiang was eighteen when he stepped into Guang's shoes and opted out of school. There was no doubt in his mind at that time as to his real calling: to continue Guang's mission of saving the lives of forbidden children. Furthering his education was put on hold as he immersed himself in the timely cause while still managing to build a rather profitable mail-order musical instrument sales and repair business. He shared his mother's musical talent, but took it in a different direction. He studied the physical creation of rich sounds made by traditional Chinese wooden instruments, and then gradually expanded into new and unique instruments. He knew them from the inside-out and what was necessary to create the sought-after deep, resonant tones. Recognized for his workmanship and beautiful wood finishes, he eventually became involved in refurbishing antique instruments, including pianos, thanks to his mother. He knew there was still a lot more to learn about pianos and the valuable old wooden instruments, but he would have to go back to school. Guo was the encouragement he needed...plus the fact that he now had more time.

He had more time because "things were changing." Guo and her contacts in Beijing told him that there were fewer and fewer babies that needed to be rescued, thanks to *new technology*.

The words: "new technology" literally meant new knowledge and equipment for parents, doctors, and the government. There were procedures being put into use for "regulating" births in keeping with the one-child-per-family mandate.

The pictures Guo showed him were disturbing – machines in hospitals, clinics, and even mobile units in vans. A machine could be rolled right next to a woman's bedside, hooked up within minutes, and a moving picture on the screen above would discern the gender of her child.

It was touted as a good thing if it was a first (legal) child. The parents could determine right then whether to keep it and celebrate the joys of parenthood, or abort it if they wished. If abortion was chosen, it was just a simple injection or medical procedure to "fix the problem." Either way, it was their decision. There were no more surprises, no worrying, no emotional drains of having to make a decision after a baby was born.

If it was a second (forbidden) child, however, the options were different – apply for an exemption and pay the tax or undergo abortion, willingly or enforced.

That's the way it was now in the larger population cities, she told him. Some remote areas still offered hope for those who were willing to move from the city and change their way of living for the sake of keeping their second child, but it was an option embraced by very few. It was simply easier to do what was right for the country, dispose of the unnecessary child, and continue in their known and accepted life style. Qiang's village was somewhere in between the busyness of Beijing and remote country life. His village was too small to have such a machine, but not small enough to hide an illegal newborn. Over all, births of forbidden children were dropping steadily as more and more couples agreed with the one-child-per-family law for the good of the country and turned to mechanized birth control and prevention.

So with more time on his hands, a growing business, the desire to continue his education, plus wanting to be closer to Guo, Qiang thought more and more about moving to Beijing now rather than waiting until after he and Guo were married. Moving his studio presented a lot of details to work out, but thoughts of a new life were tugging at him. After all, he told himself, he was not indispensable in the mission for saving the children in his village; there were at least two others who were willing and capable. The need for a "child executioner" was definitely dwindling...

   ...but it wasn't over yet – and it wasn't tonight!

   A young couple was about to bring their second child into the world. Their first was a healthy son, so whether the new baby was a boy or girl, it had to be taken away. He readied himself for the pending delivery, only the second in many months. The routine seldom varied. If it was a boy, Qiang would quietly assure the father that his son was being taken to an orphanage; then he would deliver the baby to a holding room at the hospital clinic. It was out of his hands after that, as there were still legal adoption applications within China for sons. Although such applications were becoming fewer every year, homes and adoptive parents were still being found for sons.

   Legal applications for girls, however, were rare within China. Adoptions of girls were transacted almost exclusively for couples outside of China, and even those were decreasing. "Disposal" was quicker and easier as the orphanages were overcrowded. Well known was the practice in orphanages of placing several baby girls in one crib with a single bottle of milk. Only the strongest one would survive. It was cruel by some standards, but considered effective as a form of self-elimination.

   So if the baby was a girl, no words would be spoken. Qiang would take her from the father and quickly make his way toward the hill north of the village. While family mourned either quietly or loud enough to be heard throughout the village, Qiang would deliver the baby to safety. She would then be tunneled through their illegal but workable system to waiting parents outside the country.

He personally hoped that tonight's birth would be a boy so he could take him to the clinic and not have to make that heart-wrenching trek up the hill – the scene that was supposed to educate villagers about the consequences of bringing a forbidden child into the world.

That was the visible and invisible routine in place for many years in his village. It hadn't changed.

What did change, however, was the increasing presence of government soldiers in their village. For quite a while, Qiang felt he was being watched. Their province had a new governor; the previous governor left abruptly and without explanation. It was reported that the new governor was a man of modern ideas who had little compassion for those who defied the laws of the country. Qiang knew he had to be careful; there could be "different" eyes following him tonight.

Wu Liang knew the dangers as well as she waited for him in the cave.

"It is time," came a hushed voice from outside his door.

The evening was chilly. He chose to wear his loose-fitting coat in case the baby was scantily wrapped and needed to be slipped down inside. It was a lesson he learned from his first rescue when he was handed a baby girl wrapped in nothing more than a thin cloth. He had to hold her tight to his chest for protection against the cold. He remembered his feeling of helplessness as he tried to keep the shivering infant warm from the time she was handed to him to the time it took it took to get to the top of the hill. He now had a special coat with a neatly folded baby blanket tucked in an inside pocket if he needed it.

He walked into the village where an anxious father and another man waited outside a house. His gaze was non-engaging as he bid the men good evening and sat on an empty step. Speaking no more, he stared into the darkness, waiting. This was the part of his mission that was personally disturbing – enduring the quiet scorn of family and friends and the judgmental observance of neighbors – some in agreement with the removal of an illegal child, others sympathetic to the family.

The cry of a newborn baby broke the uneasy silence. The father disappeared into the house, emerging minutes later with a tiny baby girl wrapped in a thin blanket. Here was the hardest part of all – reaching out and physically taking the child from a tearful father while listening to sobs coming from inside. He turned and walked north, head down, with the baby cradled in his arm.

His pace quickened as he left the village, anxious to get the familiar stretch of lonely road between the village and the bottom of the hill behind him. He took the extra blanket from inside his coat and wrapped it over and around the thin blanket swaddling the infant.

It was the night of a quarter moon, giving just enough light to distinguish the way before him, yet enough darkness to blend his presence into the night sky. His coat was dark, further shrouding his body. As the lights of the village faded behind him, he started feeling easier about his mission and "what could have been," but his false sense of security was shattered halfway to the hill.

Suddenly, his shadow stretched out ahead of him, created by the lights of an approaching vehicle. Cars and trucks seldom drove on this road at any time, and certainly never at night. It was more of a worn-down path than a road, created mostly by pedestrian and bicycle traffic.

Knowing the vehicle was coming for him, Qiang stepped aside and stopped as it got near, instinctively shielding the baby from the lights with his arm as she started to cry. It was an army truck. Doors opened. He could see the silhouettes of soldiers on the other side of the spotlight as he stood in its circle. Two soldiers approached, one slightly behind the other, with guns drawn.

"Who are you and what are you doing out here this time of night?" demanded the soldier in front. "What is that you're carrying?"

What am I carrying? he thought to himself. For a few seconds, his reaction was purely cynical...and wisely silent as one of the soldiers checked him over for weapons. *What does he think I'm carrying – a load of wood that cries!?* Other thoughts raced through his mind in those seconds. *And who are these guys trying to kid? They know exactly who I am, what just transpired, and where I'm going...but I have to play their game! This is it!*

It was the showdown he anticipated happening, but at the same time dreaded. He knew he could very well be caught between the army loyal to the new governor and the established system for disposal of forbidden children that was recognized and accepted by the former governor.

How much do they know? How much are they guessing? Do they only know about me or have they learned about others? Has one of our people been interrogated and coerced into talking? **God, please help me protect this baby and Wu.**

Qiang knew he had to be truthful; his activity was well known. He adjusted the baby in his arm to a different position until she stopped crying. "My name is Qiang Ming. I am on my way to the top of the hill straight ahead to dispose of an illegal child."

"Why? Is this your child?"

"No. It is a service I assumed from a man who died several years ago – a man who wished to save distraught parents in our village from having to do such a task themselves. It is an unpopular duty, but one that is necessary to control the population of our town, our province and our country."

"A service you assumed from another man? Who appointed this other man and you for this service? Was it our former governor?"

Qiang's cynicism kicked back in. *I thought so – control! New regime versus old!* "I have no instructions from our former governor," he responded. "I do it because of the law of our country and because I feel compassion for parents in our village who might otherwise have to decide for themselves how to dispose of a forbidden child."

When a flashlight suddenly appeared, shining directly in his face just inches away, Qiang could clearly see the unmistakable look of intentional intimidation in the face of the soldier. There was a silent standoff as the soldier held his stance and continued glaring into Qiang's face. Qiang did not flinch; he looked straight ahead, trying hard to squelch rising anger against *"this arrogant upstart of a would-be tyrant!"*

The child started to whimper, again becoming restless in the cradle of his arm. He moved her up against his shoulder, steadfastly protective, as he steeled his mind and body against whatever might be coming at him next. Slowly, the light was lowered.

"Your bundle of joy is getting anxious to meet her doom," the soldier joked. "Get in. We will drive you. Then I will accompany you to wherever you are going. I want to see how you handle the disposal."

"I am going to the path at the bottom of that hill," Qiang responded, nodding toward the north. "It is about a twenty-minute steep walk from there up to a cliff where she will be dropped into a ravine. That is what everyone knows and it is very visible on a clear night to those in the village. If you wish to come with me, of course you may do so. But it is not a good path at night for someone who is not familiar with it."

"I think I can handle a twenty-minute uphill walk and I can see very well. My instructions are to accompany you."

I thought so, Qiang reassured himself, trying to gauge how much more the soldier really knew or suspected. He climbed into the back seat of the truck where a third soldier was sitting with gun drawn. He could feel the adrenalin rising in his body as his emotions ricocheted between anger, panic and survival, trying to anticipate what was going to happen. *God! Please show me what to do!*

They arrived at the bottom of the hill in minutes. Qiang got out and headed toward the footpath with the soldier right behind him. "I would recommend you stay directly behind me," Qiang instructed. "If you walk where I walk, you should be safe."

"I fully <u>intend</u> to stay right behind you," came the sarcastic reply.

He thought about Wu, who was waiting in the cave. Would she notice that there was someone in back of him as she watched through the crevice? She is aware of the danger, Qiang reasoned, but they would only be visible to her for less than a minute. If she appeared at the top, her presence would expose their entire operation. Then what would happen? He shuddered to think about what that might be.

He thought about possible alternatives. What would he do if Wu saw them and *did not* come out? He would then have to decide whether to sacrifice this baby for the good of the cause or turn on the soldier and introduce him to his own doom. Then what? Maybe he could tell the others that he slipped, but that would add suspicion and bring more soldiers up the hill tomorrow to retrieve the body; they would probably discover the cave.

No matter how he figured it, nothing could possibly work. He knew someone had to die! There was no other way!

They were past the point where Wu either saw or did not see that he had company. He was feeling imminent doom, when......

"**Whoa**!" came a sudden panicked cry and the sound of sliding stones from in back of him.

Qiang turned in time to see the soldier trying to regain his footing on loose stones. He had stepped too close to the edge and was skidding back down the narrow path toward the edge where he would almost surely perish on the rocks below. Instinctively, Qiang dug in his foot, reached out with his free hand, and grabbed the soldier's flailing arm, yanking him back onto the path. They both fell backward, but onto solid ground. While the baby was safe in his protective arm, the sleeve of Qiang's other arm was torn. He felt the sting of a scrape from stones on his bared arm.

The soldier's coat sleeve was ripped wide open from a jagged rock on the edge of the path that had momentarily slowed his trajectory toward empty air and the rocks below. Blood was quickly soaking through his coat and dripping onto the ground.

Qiang laid the baby on the ground and pulled the soldier's sleeve open to assess the wound; it was deep. "Take your coat off so I can bind your arm," he told him. "It's the only way to stop the bleeding."

The soldier did as directed while Qiang unwrapped the baby from her outer blanket, hastily applying it as a tourniquet to the wounded arm. The bleeding subsided almost immediately.

"We are only minutes from the top where I can fulfill my mission. Sit here until I get back. I can't carry the baby and help you as well; it would be dangerous for both of us."

"I understand. Continue with your mission and I will wait for you here."

Qiang hurriedly picked up the crying infant and headed for the meeting spot. Would Wu be there? If not, what would he do?

She was, but stayed hidden until she was sure Qiang was alone. She heard voices and knew there was trouble. Qiang was greeted with the usual bag of rocks in one hand and the offer of a pistol in the other. He held a finger to his lips as a "hush" signal, took the bag of rocks, and exchanged it for the trembling, half-wrapped, half-naked crying baby. Wu pocketed the pistol and quickly disappeared into the cave with a warm blanket and bottle of milk to keep the child from crying.

When the debris hit the bottom of the ravine in the cold, quiet night air, the silence was perfect.

The soldier wobbled to a semi-standing position as Qiang returned.

"Stay still. I don't want to lose you now," Qiang ordered to the ashen-faced young soldier. "It's going to be a slow trip down; you've lost a lot of blood. Just hang onto me with your good arm so we can walk side by side. We will move sideways through the narrow areas."

When they emerged at last onto flat ground, Qiang loosened his grip on the soldier, who now insisted he could walk by himself.

As he started to stumble forward, however, Qiang grabbed hold of him again. The waiting soldiers pulled their guns.

"No, no. It is alright. I slipped near the top and Qiang saved my life as I was about to go over the edge. Help me into the back seat. Qiang, sit in front and show us the way to the hospital. Follow Qiang's directions."

Su-Li was worried. The familiar wail from the village two nights ago instinctively made her look toward the northern hill a short time later. There it was, just as expected – the silhouette of her son against the sky.

No! There were two silhouettes! It was a dark night, harder than usual to see, but she was pretty sure she saw two people going up and coming down. It was a much longer time than it normally took. Something was wrong. It pulled her out of her self-established comfort zone as she waited anxiously the next day and night for news. There was nothing.

Should I get in my car and go to his apartment or to his studio? No, she decided. *If he is in trouble, my presence could make it worse.* "*I am not in charge,*" she reminded herself.

She laid down a second night and tried to sleep, but a quiet knock at the door brought her upright in an instant. She almost didn't see Mulan standing outside in all dark clothes.

"Mulan! What is happening? Are you alright? Is Qiang alright?"

"I do not know about Qiang, my friend, although I am worried about him as you are...and for Wu also. She has not returned from the cave. Shing is staying with me and I left him alone to come here for just a few minutes.

"I have another concern to tell you that is disturbing. One of the members of our house church visited me tonight. When she saw Shing was with me, she asked about my garden as an excuse to talk outside. She was told that our new governor is searching out all the churches, big and small, to make sure they have legal permission to hold services. The government is blaming religion for creating recent disturbances. They are calling religion a weapon of dissidents, so all churches that are not approved have to register immediately or be destroyed. The army is enforcing their compliance, and the elders of our village are personally being held responsible for any illegal churches. That includes house churches. Anyone holding religious meetings in their homes are to cease at once or be imprisoned or..."

"What are you going to do, Mulan?"

"I am more concerned about your situation, Su-Li. Our small house church is much less recognizable than your large one; and we might be able to continue after a while if we are careful. But I know you have a Bible study tomorrow night and a lot of people attend. I also have to believe that your leaders are here under a different agreement than being missionaries, as missionaries are forbidden. Regardless of the reason, they could be in great danger if your church is discovered. No one knows which ones the government has already identified, but we are trying to warn as many of the other churches as possible for the sake of their safety.

I offered to contact you. Please tell your leaders and as many others as you possibly can."

"I know where our missionary family lives and will go to them tonight."

"Be careful, Su-Li. I will let you know if I hear anything from Wu or Qiang."

"Thank you, my friend. You be careful also."

She started to get in her car, but decided that car traffic at night through the business sector would be suspicious. She lifted her bicycle from the porch and rode quickly toward Harry and Evelyn's house, turning onto their road just in time to see an army vehicle pulling out of their driveway and coming toward her. She slowed down and tried to act casual as she moved over to the side of the road, looking away from the lights, purposely not making eye contact with the driver. Her eyes instead caught a glimpse of the passengers in the back seat – Harry and Evelyn, with Kate sitting between them.

She froze. Should she turn around and go back home? What if the soldiers decide to return and question her? How would she explain herself? Young Kate would undoubtedly try to speak to her or wave and she would have to admit knowing Harry and Evelyn. No, it would be better if she just kept going...somewhere. Her heart was pounding as she continued, trying to maintain a steady pace. A movement caught her eye as she rode by Harry and Evelyn's house – another vehicle was coming from the back of the house toward the street.

Moments later she was in the headlights of the second vehicle coming up in back of her. The lights brightened. Once again, she moved to the side of the road, hoping it would go by. It did, then pulled in front of her and stopped. Fear gripped her as she straddled her bicycle, waiting for the two soldiers who were walking toward her.

"God, please help me. Please give me the words to say."

"Where are you going at this time of night, madam?"

Where *could* she be going? The only place she could possibly be going in this direction would be Wu's studio building or Qiang's apartment...neither of which she wanted to divulge. She started to open her mouth to say something that she had not thought of yet, trusting for the words to come, when one of the soldiers spoke out abruptly:

"I recognize you! Aren't you the music teacher from Hua Zi's village? Didn't we deliver a piano to your son's studio a short distance from here?"

"Why, yes! I am Teacher Ming from Professor Zi's school. How kind of you to remember – although it would be rather hard to forget that heavy piano!"

"I remember it well! What are you doing here in this village?"

"I teach in Professor Zi's village, but I live here."

"And why are you out so late?"

"My son was not feeling well when I saw him several days ago. For some reason, I just felt that I should make sure he is alright. He lives alone and sometimes I think he does not take good care of himself so I..."

Her explanation was interrupted by laughter.

"I guess it is a mother's privilege to worry about her child, even at his age! Would you like us to put your bicycle in the back and give you a ride to your son's house?"

"That is a very generous offer, but I was actually having second thoughts about visiting him this late at night and thinking that I should turn around and go home. If I come to his door now, I would probably cause him more worry than good. I will go back home and perhaps visit him tomorrow."

"Let us take you home then. You really should not be riding around in the dark like this on a bicycle with no reflectors. It is dangerous."

With no logical way or reason to decline the offer, Su-Li stepped away from her bicycle and smiled politely as the soldiers strapped it onto the back of their vehicle and helped her step up into the back seat. *I wonder what the neighbors will think about this if they happen to be looking out,* she thought. *Hopefully I will be able to look back at this someday with amusement.*

Thankfully, her offer of tea and cakes was declined as the soldier lifted her bicycle onto the porch and bid her a good evening.

She collapsed into her chair in total frustration. There was nothing she could do about *anything* – no way to find out about what was happening with Qiang and Wu, no way to find out about Harry, Evelyn, and Kate, no way to warn any of her congregation. She thought about what had just happened – a situation that **could have been disastrous**! She remembered Qiang's words that he spoke so often about *who* was in charge...and it was not her! There was one thing she could do, however – get on her knees and pray!

"They know about our church, God, and they've got Harry and Evelyn and Kate. I was foolish to think I could just go out and take things into my own hands without You. Will I ever learn to trust in you first and then listen or watch for your guidance? I could have made things even more dangerous tonight by saying the wrong words. Thank you for protecting me and those I could have harmed.

"Please spread your protection over Qiang and Wu and that little baby and over Harry and Evelyn and Kate and all of the people in our church. Please keep us from having to become a government church to survive. All we want to do is worship You in peace. Why does it have to be dangerous? Why can't we just be free to worship You and study Your word? Why do we have to hide? Please help us!"

She lingered on her knees, head buried in her hands, not wanting to move, *waiting for something to happen,* but nothing did. She went back to bed, but sleep was impossible.

It was almost morning when she heard another soft knock on the door, Qiang's voice quietly calling her, and the familiar shuffle of his feet as he kicked his shoes off in the corner of the kitchen. A heavy weight was lifted from her shoulders – Qiang was here and safe! But something wasn't right. This was the time he would usually be leaving her house, not arriving. She was always glad to see her son *at any time*, but this morning there was an uneasiness in the air.

"I came for tea and conversation," he said with a tired voice and a half-smile as he sank into his big chair.

"You have been busy, my son; and I was worried, but you probably already knew that. Please rest while I get you some tea and something to eat. Then you can tell me what is happening. We do need to talk! Is Wu alright?"

"Yes and no," he answered.

She didn't like the sound of that. *Why is it taking forever for the water to get hot?* Finally, she and the tea tray were ready to make their way to the sitting room...where Qiang was now sound asleep. Obviously, sleep was needed! She covered him with a blanket and went back to bed, hoping to get a little sleep herself.

The street noise woke them up hours later. They were both ready at last for much needed breakfast and conversation.

"Where is Wu? Who was on the hill with you? Why were you there so long? What..."

Qiang smiled at his impetuous and often impatient mother. He glanced over at a wooden sign on the wall that his father gave her years ago with tongue-in-cheek:

Patience is a Virtue,
But Not One of Mine!

But they would not have wished her any other way!

"Wu is still in the cave and safe, Mother, but first let me tell you the big picture rather than pieces. Our mission's tunnel is in danger. Do you remember when I told you about delivering the children from the cave to a home about a hundred and fifty kilometers away and then turning them over to a man and two women?"

"Yes, I remember."

"Well, the man died suddenly a few weeks ago when his car crashed into a tree. It was said that he was driving at high speed, although no one knows why he would have been doing such a thing. His wife and sister, who are somewhat elderly, cannot physically carry on his mission to deliver children to the next safe house which, as you know, is where Guo lives. They are relatives of Guo's family. But even if the women did have another car, neither of them drive. Guo could go to them, of course, but hesitates because she feels the house is being watched. I did not know until last week when I traveled to Beijing to visit Guo that the child one of our people took to them months ago is still at their house. The two women are continuing to take care of her until we think of a solution.

"That is our first problem. Secondly, that means we have no place to take the child we rescued two nights ago who is still in the cave with Wu. We came extremely close to being discovered when you saw me going up the hill and coming down again with another person. I sensed I was being watched in the village, which was confirmed when I got about halfway to the hill and was confronted by soldiers.

"As for my company going up the hill, one of the soldiers insisted on going with me to see how I disposed of the child. Wu and I were in a very bad situation, but somehow...amazingly, it all worked out. The soldier slipped and almost tumbled off the hill before we got to the top and tore his arm up. I put a tourniquet on it and convinced him to stay where he was, so I was able to get the child to Wu. I had to help the soldier back down the hill, but at least he was convinced I tossed the baby to her death. That's as close as I ever want to get to having our operation exposed. Anyway, the soldier's arm is healing and he insists on letting the governor know of my heroic deed in saving his life. He thinks we are now best friends.

"Meanwhile, Wu is still in the cave with the child, and I dare not go back even if the safe house was operational and I had a place to take her. We cannot contact Wu, of course, but we have a plan to follow should something like this ever happen: She is supposed to wait three days and then try to bring the child back to the village when there are a lot of people around and they can blend in. If that doesn't feel safe, on the fourth day another person will casually travel to the cave by the far route that you and father and I took, and bring the child back to a temporary safe house in the village.

"My guess is that the government spies were watching me, not the hill. But since I was proclaimed a hero and my mission verified, there is probably no one watching me or the hill anymore. But Wu doesn't know that so she will probably wait until this afternoon to try to bring the child to the safe house. If we can get the baby there, she can remain hidden until we figure things out.

"In the meantime, Shing is staying with Mulan until Wu can return home."

"How can I help, Qiang?"

"There is nothing you can do, Mother, that would not be dangerous for you."

"Why would it be dangerous for me? I am not known in this cause except for my relationship to you."

"It is not your relationship with me that is risky right now, Mother. It is your relationship with your church. I am almost certain it is being demolished!"

"What?! How do you know this?"

"I saw big bulldozers going in that direction – toward your road...and there is only one building on that road big enough to require a bulldozer – your church building. There is nothing you or anyone can do; you need to stay away. You are widely recognized as being my mother and I, in turn, widely recognized as disposing of children. If you are tied to both the church and me, even though the perception is I was banished from your house before father died, my mission might come under scrutiny. Disposal of children is in conflict with church teachings. Even though I was supposedly banished, it might raise questions, more suspicion, and danger for others."

It was another feeling of frustration and helplessness for Su-Li. She feared for the safety of Harry, Evelyn and Kate. She realized her own vulnerability in being recognized for several reasons and, last night, she barely escaped a perilous predicament by not thinking of the consequences of her actions. She remembered the haunting wails of a mother three nights ago who will never know that her child was saved from death. She thought about two babies with no place to go and the people caring for them. She worried about Qiang – his situation was much more perilous than when Guang did it. She knew he was worried about Guo and her family. Then there was Wu – if she was discovered, Qiang would be implicated through sharing their studio building! Never had she felt so afraid, so concerned. Many people were in danger and for many reasons!

"When I stopped by Mulan's house to assure her that Wu was safe and would probably be back home today," Qiang continued, "she told me about visiting you earlier. That was before she knew of the discovery and demolition of your church. She was horrified to think she may have placed you in danger, so I was relieved to find you here and safe. I will let her know."

Now it was Qiang's turn to hear of a serious situation – the one his mother somehow managed to emerge unscathed from last night. He was not surprised to hear that the soldier recognized her and connected her with him and the piano...their feathered hair feature always seemed to make them memorable. What *did* concern him, however, was the soldiers delivering his mother and the bicycle to her doorstep. Now they knew where she lived.

After hearing his mother's story, he was even more insistent that she should do nothing...not even leave the house! She agreed.

Qiang left in the full light of day, quickly and unobtrusively blending into the street traffic, hoping to attract no one's attention as he headed toward his studio to wait for Wu.

Wu traveled to the village mid-afternoon with the baby strapped to her back in a traditional mei-tai carrier used by many mothers with small children. Owners of the temporary safe house were waiting for her while others casually strolled through the neighborhood to make sure she was not being followed. All was well...she was given the signal to go in. With the baby in good hands, Wu was looking forward to picking up Shing, going home, and resting. But first, she wanted to stop by the studio where she was pretty sure Qiang would be waiting for her. He was. She wanted to find out about the soldier who was with him on the hill. She caught a glimpse of a uniform as they approached so she knew the other person was a soldier, but the rest of the story was even more amazing. She laughed when Qiang told her he was now considered a hero and scheduled to be brought to the governor for formal recognition of some kind for saving the soldier's life!

The conversation turned serious again, however, when Qiang told her about the demolition of her previous building – discovered to be an illegal church that was registered as a produce processing market, with all the paperwork handled by his father, Cheng. Also disturbing was the public crushing of her beautifully-made glass cross that hung inside the door. Her indirect involvement with real estate, her art business, people from the church, and ultimately her husband Guang and his mission, could raise many questions. Wu's skin bristled as she sensed a net of suspicion settling over them.

There was nothing they could do, however, except continue with business as usual, try to remain unnoticed, and hope no more illegal children would be born for a while.

It was early in the day when the army vehicle arrived at Qiang's apartment to transport him to the Office of the Governor. With his new "best friend" Zhang personally accompanying him, they pulled up to the front door of the stately building and made their way to a large office at the back. They were personally greeted by the governor, who read aloud a decree of heroism and formally presented it to Qiang on behalf of the provincial government and the Peoples Republic of China. Then the governor stepped aside as Qiang was honored with a salute from Zhang and a contingent of military personnel. Offering a nod of respect in return, Qiang accepted an invitation from Zhang to join him and several of the officers for lunch. It was exquisite from the pouring of first tea to the offering of a fine after-dinner cigar and smoking room. As neither Zhang nor Qiang smoked, they opted instead for dessert. For the first time since their episode on the hill path, Zhang and Qiang found themselves alone.

"Zhang, I appreciate what you have done, and I am very honored, but I do not feel worthy of being treated as a hero."

"You are *my* hero, Qiang. I was doing my job as a soldier in command, with my head full of carrying out my duty instead of watching the path like you told me to do. You could easily have let me go over the edge of the cliff. I know that. You didn't have to grab my arm and risk your own life. You could have thrown yourself off balance and gone over the cliff as well. Why did you do it? Why *did* you save me?"

It was a question Qiang anticipated. He thought about possible answers but, after Zhang's truthful analysis of their situation, the answers didn't fit. He was not expecting anything so mature to come from this brash young man.

"Well, it wasn't because I really liked you!" Qiang said with an amusement he felt he could share with his new best friend.

Zhang laughed. "Yeah, I was kind of a pain in the backside, wasn't I?"

"Kind of. But you were doing your job and so was I. As you probably know, I am referred to as the 'child executioner' in my village, although it is not a title I enjoy. I would prefer a job of saving lives rather than taking them. Maybe saving your life was a privilege I was allowed to have as some sort of restitution."

Conversation lapsed into reflective silence as they finished the last of their dessert. "Qiang, I…"

Qiang waited for the rest of the sentence, but it didn't come.

"You what?"

"Well...it's an eerie feeling to come close to death and be pulled back. I've done a lot of thinking since that night – you know, about myself and who I am and who I should be. It's like I have been given another chance by...well, another chance. As you said, maybe like some kind of restitution."

What is this guy trying to say? Qiang wondered. *Is he trying to tell me he actually believes in some kind of special calling or answering to a higher power? He's supposed to be an atheist! Or is he trying to find out where* my *loyalties are?*

"And what conclusions have you reached, Zhang?"

Another reflective silence. "I haven't really...and please don't misunderstand – I am not a coward who is afraid to die for my country or for what I believe in, but that night on the hill when I stared death in the face, it was an awakening. I've been asking myself since then what it is that I am really willing to die for? What do I truly believe in? For some reason, I keep thinking about those crazy students in Tiananmen Square back in '89 facing off with tanks and tear gas bombs. They were willing to die for their cause. Why? Were they brave or just plain foolish? How do you or I or anyone know how important – or unimportant a cause is? What is meaningful today may not be significant at all tomorrow. We only have one life to give for what we believe in. I just don't know what I believe in anymore. I'm sorry to be rambling on, Qiang. You probably think I'm a bit loony, right?"

"No, I don't."

Their conversation was interrupted by the return of the smokers. Their vehicle was waiting; it was time to leave.

The arrival of electricity in their village brought with it the expected "new technology" machine, with emphatic instructions from the governor for its use. Being tested was not an option. It was a requirement for all women who were with child, suspected to be with child, or in some cases just being of child-bearing age. The only babies *allowed to be born* were those who were legal and wanted.

Qiang was out of a job!

Other changes arrived with electricity – lights on the main streets and in some homes and buildings, and a scattering of computers, especially for students and businessmen. It didn't take long, however, for computer users to realize that PCs (personal computers) were not personal. The eyes and ears of the government came with them!

The baby tunnel was still in a dilemma - there were two infants caught up in the stalled rescue system. As each day passed, it was getting more difficult to hide the presence of a newborn at the village safe house. Then there was the question of what to do with the months-old child still at the first delivery location between their village and Beijing. How could they get these two little girls moving again toward the arms of waiting parents? It seemed impossible – until Guo came up with the solution, albeit out of necessity to solve a different dilemma.

She and Qiang were preparing to begin their lives together. With her graduation just weeks away, wedding plans were also being made. Qiang was searching for a suitable (and affordable) location in Beijing for his business; soon they would be looking for an apartment. Everything seemed to be falling into place – until they got to the guest list for the wedding!

Who from Qiang's village should be invited? The stigma of "child executioner" was still fresh in the minds of its people, even though "disposal" was not being carried out any more. That meant that whoever was invited to the wedding as a friend of Qiang's would be suspected of having involvement with the disposal of children, or at least being sympathetic to it. They would be *guilty by association*.

Certainly Su-Li's friends would question receiving an invitation to Qiang's wedding, even though they loved Su-Li. If Qiang was her banished son, why would she be participating in a wedding for him. Was she now welcoming him back into her home? Would it mean that she accepted his role in the disposal of children?

Could they invite Su-Li's friend, Mulan – Guang's mother, the woman Su-Li used to shun? Guang took Su-Li's daughter and dropped her to her death. Is she now defending his mother? How could that be? Is Su-Li now in agreement with the government and what Guang did?

Could they invite Wu Liang and Shing, who had so far remained unidentified? Their relationship to Mulan would probably be exposed.

And that was just Qiang's friends and side of the family!

What about Guo's grandmother and aunt, who lived in the first destination safe house? Would they be able to attend the wedding? Who would take care of the baby who was still marooned in their home? Her grandmother and aunt were special people...they *had to be* at the wedding!

It was customary to have part of the wedding celebration at the bride's home. Guo's family was pretty sure their house was being watched. Would their guests be monitored? They discontinued their meetings but still had to be careful not to expose identities.

The logistics of who to invite and who not to invite were playing havoc with their day of celebration...until Guo came up with the perfect solution:

"Why don't we choose a place in Beijing that is popular for weddings, Qiang – a lovely restaurant or garden, and invite people to come there? We will keep everything private and only include those who are involved with the children's cause or know about it. We can have one of the "unknowns" pick up grandmother and auntie and the baby, and the couple from the safe house in your village can come and bring their baby. Then we will have the people further down the tunnel attend as well, and they can simply switch caregivers and the new ones can take the babies home with them.

"Think about it. We won't have to send out formal invitations – they will all be verbal, like spreading the word about a party at the university! We will have a good time with everyone who is there because they will all be workers, relatives or friends who

140

share our commitment. The babies will be on their way to new homes, and grandmother and auntie and the couple from your village will have their lives back. We don't know for sure whose houses are being watched, but we will draw less attention by going out like it was any other normal day than if we were to have a house full of visitors. And when it is all over, we will be married!"

It was so simple, it was beautiful...as long as everything went along as expected. As much as Guo's parents said they would have preferred a larger and more formal wedding for their only daughter, under the circumstances, her proposal was well received.

They planned the wedding right after Guo's graduation. It was a beautiful day with all of the emotions, joys, and happiness of any wedding except it included likely and unlikely guests brought together by a common bond. Everyone had fun, ate well, and shared in the festivities of the traditional Chinese celebration. When it was over, the babies were on their way to new homes and the caregivers returned to their everyday lives. Qiang, Guo, and their families met again later at their underground church in Beijing for a private Christian ceremony.

Qiang and Guo found their perfect two-bedroom apartment on the outskirts of the city, just five kilometers from the building they rented for Qiang's mail-order business. Now all that was left to do was get Qiang's business moved to Beijing. Everything was settling into place in less time than they had anticipated.

Moving Qiang's business was the sad part for Su-Li. She knew he was going to be leaving, but it was happening way too fast. At least when he was in their village, she could see him once in a while.

Guo sensed the sad feelings of her new mother-in-law. Su-Li was a busy person with lots of friends, but her husband was gone and now her only child was moving away. As much as she tried to hide it, there was an aura of loneliness hanging over Su-Li like a heavy cloud. *She has to be feeling abandoned*, Guo realized.

While Qiang was loading his car with boxes of instrument parts and she and Su-Li were packing dishes and utensils from his small studio kitchen, Guo spoke words from her heart: "Mrs. Ming...no, wait. I can call you mother now if it is agreeable with you."

The name "mother" instead of "Mrs. Ming" brought her somewhat out of the darkness she had been in all morning. Yes, she was now a mother-in-law, and Guo was the perfect mate that any mother could want for her son. But the reality of Qiang being gone *was* beginning to hit her hard. Everything was happening so fast – the graduation party, the wedding, moving the homeless babies, finding an apartment, and now Qiang's business getting moved. Su-Li hadn't thought about much of anything but the whirlwind of activity for weeks until today...moving day.

She stopped and looked at her new daughter-in-law. "Why, of course, Guo. I am honored to have you call me mother."

"Thank you...Mother, and I do not mean that as an assumed form of address that comes from marrying your son because if I could choose my mother-in-law from anyone I know, you would be my number one choice. You have been through a lot and I truly admire your strength. I know you would love to have your own daughter standing here right now, helping your son pack, but that cannot be, so I hope to fill that void as much as I can.

"I also know you must be sad because Qiang is moving from the village, but you have my promise that distance will not make us distant. I am now part of your family and I believe in closeness. We will be here often and hope you will visit us in Beijing whenever you can. We are decorating your room in pastels."

What beautiful, honest words from her new daughter-in-law! Guo's reference to Xiu-Su was unexpected; she had not been thinking along those lines through all the weeks of busyness. The personal expression of empathy from the young woman standing before her touched her heart. She walked over and embraced the newest member of her family. "Welcome to our world and our family, Guo my daughter! I am looking forward to spending time with you and Qiang, whether in my home or yours."

She paused and looked intently into Guo's concerned face. "I know my son is happy, Guo, and you are the reason. Happiness for Qiang is long overdue, and seeing him smile and hearing him laugh warms my heart. And yes, I know Xiu-Su and Syaran are gone from me forever on this earth, but I have you and Qiang, for which I am extremely thankful. I will pray for peace and happiness for both of you every day."

Qiang walked back into the room and couldn't imagine why his wife and mother were both wiping tears from their eyes. Should he ask? No, he decided. If he knew his impetuous, caring mother and his considerate, loving wife, they would iron out whatever it was. Some things he didn't need to know.

###

It was months after the destruction of her church when Su-Li finally felt safe to venture in that direction. The rubble was still there as a reminder of what happens to unregistered churches. She was warned not to look for anything in the piles of debris – just ride by on her bicycle, as many curious villagers did. Yet her heart ached when she saw a piece of the old piano protruding from one of the piles. Everything was demolished and bulldozed together – bricks, wood, furniture, Bibles, music stands, baptismal font – their entire church, broken and destroyed. It was a sad reminder that even though things had been quiet for many years, "freedom of religion" was still nothing more than a phrase of political rhetoric. She rode on.

Seeing the remains of her church for the first time since it was leveled brought mixed emotions. Yes, their building and its contents were gone, but the *spirit* of the church was very much alive and stronger than ever! People from their congregation were meeting quietly in small house groups – informal sessions, sharing Bibles, choosing new leaders, and continually praying for Harry and Evelyn and Kate. There was still no word from them or about them.

Their large congregation became a dozen small ones. Su-Li became part of one led by Jian, a strong supporter of their previous large church. Including herself, there were ten people – definitely the smallest church she ever attended. Jian and his wife took turns presenting Bible studies while others led in prayer and rituals. They missed the larger congregation with all of its activities, but took comfort in knowing that the rest of their members (as far as they knew) were still alive and continuing to learn and share the

144

gospel. It made them all the more determined to keep their freedom to worship strong and spreading.

Su-Li thought about the uplifting music. She missed it, but it was too risky to have music in an area where houses were so close together. Instead, they sang hymns together softly.

She thought about the destruction of the piano that Qiang spent so much time and effort to restore. She thought about the other instruments that brought so much joy to listeners...including her own set of chimes that stayed in the church from week to week. If only they could have known earlier what was coming, they would have been able to save some of the instruments as well as Bibles and music books! But she was thankful for what they did have...each other, shared Bibles, and hopefully safety.

A year later, Su-Li was invited to be one of the leaders of the house church, taking the place of Jian's wife who was now helping to take care of Jian's aging parents. Su-Li was an obvious choice because she was already a teacher. At first, she didn't feel qualified to teach the gospel, but soon realized it enriched her own learning as well. She enjoyed her new assignment more and more and was especially thankful for a prized possession given to the underground church leaders in her village from an anonymous donor – a study Bible. It dug deeper into the gospel than her regular Bible, adding new and meaningful information. She and Jian joined in meetings with other church leaders as they studied together, learned, planned lessons, and continued to teach.

SHOES IN THE RIVER

Chapter 10: A Window to the Past

2003

Once again, Su-Li's life was settling down. It was her third year as a music teacher and second year of taking her students "on the road" to other schools to sing and play. They were even invited to perform in two of the local government churches and at a wedding. It kept her busy during the week, and teaching at her small house church kept her busy on weekends.

She was up early today. It was Friday and she had her usual early appointment slot at the Volkswagen dealership on her way to school. She settled into a comfortable chair in the customer lounge and selected a magazine to read while she waited for her car to be serviced. It was a well-read, outdated, dog-eared travel magazine. With Cheng's dislike for travel, books like this were never in their home, and still weren't. Perhaps that was why she looked forward to reading them at the dealership. Beautiful pictures of far-away places, expensive jewelry, exotic foods, and luxury cars filled each page.

Oh, to visit one of those places, she thought wistfully, would be so exciting! Unlike Cheng, Su-Li knew she could very well fit into the travel scene, but she never had a reason or opportunity to leave China. Well, it was fun looking at the pictures anyway and imagining herself on one of those big cruise ships!

As she flipped through the colorful pages, caught up in thoughts of make-believe travel, one picture captured her attention. She paused a little longer to study a group of young people, obviously musicians, gathered around a beautiful grand piano.

It was an article about a symphony concert in England. There was a larger picture of the conductor and the symphony members, but it was the smaller photograph of young people next to it that drew her in. The group of ten were students – guest musicians scheduled to perform with them: "Music Students International." It elicited a vision of some of her own students performing with such a group one day. She lingered for a while longer with the opened magazine on her lap, enjoying thoughts of what such an experience might be like.

Right now, however, it was just a dream. She started to turn the page when *something out of place* drew her back into the smaller picture. There was a white spot on the hair of a young girl sitting on the piano bench. She looked closer. **Then she looked much closer!**

She was an Asian girl **with hair just like her own**...dark and slightly wavy with a rather large distinctive white "feather" on the right side of her head. It was like looking at a picture of her own younger self!

Goose bumps engulfed her entire body as an unbelievable possibility jumped off the page at her!

Could it possibly be....? *No, of course not,* she admonished herself! **But maybe...**

She stared at the picture, not able to put the magazine down, even when she was called and told her car was ready. She looked at the date on the cover – it was eight months old. "Could I *please* buy this magazine from you?" she asked the service manager. "There is something in here I am very interested in."

She didn't know what she would have done if he said no; she acted on impulse, the words just blurting out. "Oh, you can take it with you, Mrs. Ming. It's quite old. I'm sure everyone has read it."

By the time she got to school, the only thing on her mind was the picture. *How can I find out more about this concert and the music students? We have two computers here, perhaps connected to the internet, but I know schools are overseen by the government. Even if I got permission to use a computer, would it be safe? How could I explain why I want to use one? My students are too young to be considered for international concerts – I couldn't use that as a viable reason. I need help! Who can I talk to that I can trust?*

Somehow, she got through the day's lessons. But as the last child left the classroom, her attention focused only on the picture and how she could possibly find out more about Music Students International.

"God, please help me! If there is any remote possibility that this is my daughter, *please* show me what to do!"

As she drove home, she thought of everyone who might be able to help. Qiang? Maybe through the university? No, he was too new in Beijing to know many people and she did not want to jeopardize him in any way. Guo? Possibly. Wu? She didn't know.

149

"Please, God," she prayed again. ***"Please* show me the way!"**

Being the end of the work week, Su-Li spent the whole next day staring at the picture, looking at it closer with Cheng's magnifying glass. *How many people could have hair like this*, she wondered. *Maybe many, but no one I've ever known or seen. Maybe I just haven't met them yet. Maybe I'll find out that the young woman has biological parents and then I won't even have to think about it anymore! But maybe not.*

She was startled by a knock at her door. "Su-Li? Are you home? It's Huan Qu'nan. Remember me?"

Huan. Yes – the friend who was with Cheng the day he was killed...the man who took over Cheng's job and helped her and Qiang sort through all of the insurance and investment papers. "What a lovely surprise, Huan! Of course I remember you. You helped Qiang and me make sense out of all that paperwork. Please come in and let me fix you some tea."

"I've been trying to find you home for the past couple of weeks and finally had a chance to talk to one of your neighbors. She told me you are now a music teacher working in another village and I'd have to come by on a weekend if I wanted to catch up with you. It sounds like you are a busy lady now that you are driving," he said with a friendly grin as he ambled in.

Oh, that smile! How it reminded her of Cheng.

"Yes, I have definitely been busy. When your company was kind enough to give me Cheng's car, which initially I did not know what to do with, I decided it was a reason and an opportunity to learn to drive, and I'm so glad I did. It has enabled me to travel to Beijing and bring my education up to date, find a job in my field as a music teacher, and get myself to places other than this village."

"I hope you are working because you want to and not because you have to, Su-Li. I was hoping that the funds from Cheng's investments would be sufficient for you. Are they not?"

"Oh, yes, the funds are doing fine. Teaching music to children is something I always planned to do but never pursued. I just wish I would have done it sooner. The children are so precious and anxious to learn. They are a joy! Now tell me why I have the pleasure of your visit."

"It's almost embarrassing, Su-Li. You would think that a group of accountants would have no problem keeping correct books, but four years after losing Cheng, we just now discovered a mistake in our records that was with one of his investments. We kept receiving funds that we didn't think we were supposed to have and couldn't figure out who they belonged to. They were for an employee number that kept bouncing back saying there was no such person. We decided, therefore, that there must be an error within our company rather than with the brokerage firm. We went back year by year for four years and found the error – it was with Cheng. Someone had inverted two numbers in recording his employee number for a stock purchase. So the good news is that you have additional income. The bad news is that we now have more paperwork for you. If you have time now, I'll go over it with you, or I can come back when Qiang is present if you would prefer. We have several options to offer you; I just need to know how you want us to proceed."

Su-Li was astounded when she saw the figures.

"In a condensed story," Huan continued, "this is from a start-up foreign investment company that was new seven years ago and has grown considerably. But because it is from another country and Cheng is deceased, there are a lot of legal papers to fill out before the transfer can be made to you." He started to spread a collection of papers out on the table.

"Huan, this looks like something we are probably going to need your help with again. I know nothing about foreign investments and I don't think Qiang would know either, even though he is taking an economics class at the university. Do you have any advice?"

"Well, yes and no. This investment opportunity started out as an offering through our company but, after a few years of initially not performing well, our company decided to drop it and roll the funds over to other options. Cheng was one of just a few who bought shares and wanted to keep them, but he died at the same time the change took place. As a result, Cheng's contribution did not get moved to other accounts or paid out. In other words, 'it fell through the cracks,' and doubly so when his employee number was not copied correctly.

"Now this is where it gets even more complicated, Su-Li. Unfortunately, because this has not been a company option for the last four years, it cannot be straightened out through our company. It has to be considered a private investment, even though dividends have been paid to our company, if that makes any sense. But I think we have figured out a way to retrieve the funds for you without passing them through the company books...that is, assuming you wish to cash the stock in. If you don't want to cash it in, then we will need to get Cheng's name removed and your name put on the certificates. I think I have all the papers needed to make it happen either way. What you have to do is decide how you want it transacted."

"Please forgive me, Huan, for not being wiser about investments, but there is no way I am going to be able to explain all of this to Qiang without you. I know you are very busy, and I appreciate all that you have done to help us, but is there a convenient time you could talk to Qiang, perhaps in Beijing? That is where he lives now, although he and his lovely wife are going to be here Tuesday afternoon."

"I didn't know Qiang got married! Wow – a lot has happened since I was here last. Well, it would undoubtedly be easier to meet with both you and Qiang at the same time. Tuesday is fine with me, but after that I will be gone for a couple of weeks on business. Tai Ying has been working on this with me so he can meet with you after Tuesday if you need him. Do you remember Tai?"

She reluctantly allowed her mind to go back to that horrible night. "Yes. He and another man came to my house to tell me about Cheng. Tai stayed with me while the other man went to find Qiang. I remember him and his kindness. But hopefully we can get it all taken care of while you are here. Will you be able to join us for dinner?"

"Of course!" His face lit up with another smile at the invitation. "A bachelor like me would be foolish to pass up an opportunity for some good home cooking! I will see you Tuesday."

Su-Li was once again alone with her magazine and picture, and now an overload of new information from Huan. She <u>had</u> to talk to Qiang. If only she had a phone! Qiang wanted her to get one, but reception was not particularly good in their area; even worse where she worked, so she really hadn't seen much value in it. Maybe it was time to reconsider...but Wu had a phone!

Wu was just closing her door for the day when Su-Li arrived. "Wu, I am so sorry to bother you on your way home, but I need your help. I have to talk to either Qiang or Guo rather quickly and I do not have a phone...but I have both of their numbers here. Would you be kind enough to try to reach them for me?"

"Of course I will."

"No service" kept coming up on Wu's phone. She faced different ways until finally...a call went through to Guo's phone.

"Mother? Is something wrong?"

"Guo, I know you and Qiang are planning to be here Tuesday afternoon, but could you possibly come earlier? I have two very important things to discuss and they are both going to take a while.

154

A man from Cheng's company is going to join us for dinner and he needs to talk to us about one of Cheng's accounts. It's rather complicated and I don't feel comfortable making decisions like that on my own. The other thing I need to talk about is an idea."

"Qiang only has two classes on Tuesday, and they are both early morning, so yes, we can be there earlier."

"Thank you, Guo. I will see you as soon as you can get here then."

She handed the phone back to Wu with words of thanks and a determination to get a phone of her own!

Su-Li was almost bursting with pent-up anxiety, past the point of being contained, when Qiang and Guo arrived. They were barely in the house when Su-Li opened the magazine and placed it on the table in front of them, pointing to the picture. "Look at the girl sitting at the piano," she said, hardly controlling the urgency in her voice. "Look at her hair!"

Qiang looked at the picture, then picked the magazine up and examined it closer with the magnifying glass. He looked at his mother, waiting for more explanation.

"Do you think" ... she stammered... "Do you think there is any possibility it could be Xiu-Su?"

She told them about going to the car dealership, finding this magazine, trying to keep her mind on her class all day, getting home and staring at the picture the whole next day, trying to figure out how to get more information about it, Huan coming to visit her, the surprise investment, wishing she had a phone, deciding to get one...and now she needed their help.

There. Everything on her mind just spilled out of her mouth in one big, long sentence. Well, not quite everything. She continued:

"I am so glad you are here tonight to listen to Huan. If we can't get this financial thing resolved, we will have to talk to someone else or wait for two weeks until he returns from a business trip. I've invited him for dinner. I made one of your favorites so you can take some home with you. It sounds complicated but I think..."

It was only when Qiang started laughing that she realized she was rambling on at lightning speed.

"Mother, I'm sure we can figure this financial thing out, especially if we have Huan's good advice. I'm looking forward to seeing him again and introducing him to Guo. Now tell me...what are you planning to do with this picture?"

"I don't know. Please help me figure out who can help us find information about this group and this person. I can't think of anyone with a computer that I know well enough to trust. Even if I did, it would still not be wise, but *I have to know* – one way or the other!"

Qiang was silent. The women sat quietly as he walked over to the window and stared out into the late afternoon sky.

"Let's think about this for a while, Mother. We have to be careful that we don't raise any suspicions, especially about someone who is not even supposed to be alive. I agree that we do need to know, even though it is only a remote possibility, but let's figure out the best way to go about it. There could be a lot at stake here. Maybe one of us will have an idea in the next day or so of someone we can talk to. Meanwhile, why don't I come back this weekend and see what we can do about getting you a phone?

"Also," he continued, "I know how tempting it is to think about things when you are driving. Please be careful this week not to let your mind wander too much when you are on the road...just a few words of caution from your son!"

Su-Li breathed a sigh of relief. Qiang was right. She needed to focus on her students during the day and think about these other things when she was home. It was a secure feeling as always, knowing she has a sensible son with good judgment and advice.

A knock on the door announced Huan's arrival.

"Huan, come in. Dinner is going to be a little later than I planned as I got carried away with other things. Would you care for a cup of tea while we're waiting?"

157

"Thank you, Su-Li; that sounds wonderful. Ummm. It sure does smell good in here!

"Qiang, it is good to see you again...I hope you are doing well. Your mother surprised me by becoming a music teacher since the last time I was here. And now I understand you are a married man and living in Beijing!"

"Yes, only a few months ago. This is my bride, Guo." Qiang looked over at his wife as she stepped forward. "Guo, Huan is the man who took father's place after he died. He has been a good friend and valuable advisor."

Guo's response was just as surprising as Huan's as they walked toward each other and joined in a mutual embrace of old friends. "It's nice to see you again, Huan. It has been many years."

Guo smiled as she turned to address the stares of her husband and mother-in-law. "I did not know the name of the person who was going to be with us tonight, and it is a lovely surprise to see it is my dear friend, Huan. He and his wife, Gong Li, have been to my parents' home many times. They were both very active in our cause for rescuing babies. There are a lot more people involved in Beijing than there are here; we had regular meetings so everyone would know each other. I have not been to one in a long time because of school and my studies."

"Thank you, Guo," Huan continued. "Please forgive my hesitancy in speaking. I was trying to put everything together in my mind when I saw you and Qiang together. I heard you got married and am sorry I couldn't attend, but I didn't realize your husband was Qiang. So my very astute guess is that you met each other through working with the cause for children, but not at your parents' house, right? I never saw Qiang there."

"You are absolutely right. We met at my aunt and uncle's safe house outside of Beijing."

There was silence as Huan's smile faded and his face suddenly became more serious. "Su-Li, do we have a little time for some other personal words? I have been neglectful of a promise I made to Cheng and it has been bothering me for quite a while. Amazingly, this feels like the right time and the right company to discuss it."

"Yes, we have time, Huan."

With everyone seated, Huan continued. "My wife passed away a few months before Cheng did. Her sickness was a long and painful journey for her. Cheng was my best friend through all of our hardships. He not only did his own work, but much of mine as I tended to the needs of Gong Li. Without his help, I probably would have lost my job. But instead, Cheng made me look good. Never did I expect to have his job one day, and I wish it had not happened as it did. Cheng was a good co-worker and a good friend."

So that was why Cheng was late getting home so many nights, Su-Li suddenly realized! *His explanation was always that he was working after hours with Huan to get caught up.*

"Cheng not only spent a lot of time doing my job for me," Huan continued, "but he spent time with me in prayer at his old church

159

in Beijing. We prayed for Gong Li in her sickness, and for you, Su-Li, as you struggled with the loss of your children and grieving for so many years. We prayed for your peace and we prayed for comfort and peace for all the other parents and children. As Guo said, Gong Li and I were both very involved in the effort to save them. It came about after our own daughter – our second child, was taken. Unfortunately, there was no Guang or Qiang to help back then and we know she perished. Part of the healing process for us was in learning that there were people in Beijing who were starting to champion the cause of saving the discarded children. We met one such man through a mutual, caring friend, and that man encouraged our help. That was Guo's father, and we decided to join him in his mission.

"But it was because of Cheng's compassion for Gong Li and me after the loss of our daughter that he introduced us to his small Christian church in Beijing and we both converted. I cannot tell you how much it changed our lives by knowing we would someday meet the child we were not allowed to keep. Through our new church we learned and truly believed what we needed to hear – the truth about Heaven and eternal life. Right now, I know Gong Li and our daughter are together and they wait for me.

"The members of our Christian church were also very kind when Gong Li could not physically attend services. Every week someone would come to our house and bring the sermon to us and sometimes communion. It was very personal and meant a lot to both of us.

"I know Cheng honored the confidence I placed in him about our involvement in the children's rescue, especially as it was only happening in Beijing and not in your village...at least that is what we both thought. But when you got involved, Qiang, and were finally able to share this cause with your parents, it created some...some worries, let's say for your father. Cheng made me promise that if anything should happen to him, I would make sure your mother was taken care of and keep a watchful eye over you as much as possible."

He looked back at Su-Li. "I have done this indirectly, Su-Li, through following the disbursement of funds into your bank and making sure there were no change notifications, but I should have been more personally attentive. There was just no reason I could think of to come here for a visit that would not have seemed strange to you. Now I have one – this unexpected fund popping up."

Surprise number three in three days, Su-Li recalled silently. First it was finding the magazine article, then an unexpected income, and now Huan is standing here telling us of his involvement with the children's cause, already knowing Guo and her family. What else could possibly happen?

Then it struck her – Huan! Could he possibly be their connection to the outside world and the internet? She discreetly looked over at Qiang as she reached for the magazine. He nodded his approval. But it would wait until after dinner.

SHOES IN THE RIVER

Chapter 11: A Window to the Future

2003

The first item of business after dinner was what to do with the income from Cheng's foreign investment account. It came down to whether or not it should be reinvested as stock, set up as an annuity, or cashed in. Qiang had several questions, which Huan answered knowledgeably, but the final decision was up to Su-Li. Huan was prepared with the necessary forms for whatever she chose to do. She surprised them all by opting to receive the funds in a lump sum.

"What are you going to do with that much money, Mother? Did something in that travel magazine catch your eye?"

"No. I want to buy a piano."

"A piano?!"

"Yes. You were wonderful to restore that old one for my school four years ago, Qiang, and oh, how I wish you could see the smiling faces in my class whenever it is played. The children absolutely love it, and some of them are getting to be quite good with it. But it is still an old piano and getting more tired every year. We could keep it to use in the assembly room where the children could still play it, but I would love to have a new one, or at least a newer one, for the music room...for the children and for myself as well. I want to encourage my students to excel as musicians, even if it is only for their own enjoyment, but they need to have good instruments to play, especially a piano. I want to buy a new one and donate it to the school in memory of your father. After all, it was his planning that made this income possible and he loved music and children just as much as you and I do. Then I want to replace a few of the other instruments as well. That's what I want to do."

"It will be as you wish, of course, Su Li, and your choice is actually the least complicated option. It will be much easier to have the funds disbursed to you in a lump sum as Cheng's beneficiary rather than having them transferred to you from another country in a newly established investment account. This will be quick and simple and I should have a bank draft for you within a couple of weeks."

With the papers signed and tucked away in Huan's briefcase, and a nod from Qiang, Su-Li picked up the magazine. "Huan, there might be another reason that this unexpected fund has brought you here. May I show you something that Qiang and Guo and I are trying to figure out? Perhaps you can help us."

"I will help if I can."

She placed the opened book in front of him, pointing to the article about the symphony performance. "I was leafing through this magazine at the dealership last week while my car was being serviced. See the girl sitting on the piano bench? Look at her hair, and then look at my hair and Qiang's hair."

She handed him the magnifying glass, gave him time to study the picture and, as suggested, compare the unique hair "feathers" of all three. He looked back at Su-Li in puzzled astonishment.

"That young lady looks to be about the age my daughter Xiu-Su would be today," Su-Li explained. "She was taken from me the day she was born, but I know she survived and has been adopted by a family outside our country. If there is any possibility that this might be Xiu-Su...and we know it is only a remote possibility, we want to know. But we can't figure out how to go about it without bringing attention to ourselves. We don't want to expose the tunnel in any way or the safety of the dear souls who worked in it. Do you have any suggestions?"

Huan turned to the inside cover. "This is printed in the United States," he said. "It's old but not *that* old. The publishers probably still have information in their files. We can't safely contact them from here, as you know, but I could possibly research it while I am in the United States and Canada next week...if it is possible without causing raised eyebrows. I leave on Thursday and won't be able to contact you until I return, but I promise you that I will try my best to find some information. Nothing would make me happier than to reunite a parent with a lost child or a brother with a sister."

The United States and Canada! Su-Li remembered Huan mentioning a business trip, but didn't realize it was going to be out

165

of the country! All that Su-Li could think of was: *"God, you have again answered my prayer! Thank you! Thank you!"*

###

It was Huan's first trip abroad – actually, his first trip anywhere outside of Asia. He had been on planes before, but they were like toys compared with this jumbo jet!

The day-and-a-half layover in Hawaii was a great way to be introduced to the world of global travel and multiple time zone changes. What an awesome place it was – the beaches, colorful buildings, trees and lavish flowers, modern cars, exotic food. He couldn't help but laugh at the two usually very business-oriented men he was traveling with sitting on beach chairs in the sand. Li Ju and Xuegin Wong were acting like happy tourists, obviously enjoying themselves amid the circle of beautiful women in swishing grass skirts dancing in strange fashion to a ukulele. A wave of sadness swept over him as he thought of Gong Li and how she would have loved this place, especially the flowers and birds, which were her passion. And she also would have enjoyed this strange ring of fragrant flowers around her neck. It was almost five years since her death, and he still missed her terribly. It was a lonely existence without her!

He thought about his recent visit with Su-Li and remembered how her eyes got teary when they talked about Cheng. He regretted being so insensitive to her feelings and probably those of Qiang as well. He should have been more careful with his words instead of just blurting everything out about his own problems! He decided to apologize to them when he got back home. Better yet, he would

166

make an exceptional effort to find out about the girl in the picture. Somehow...he had to do this for them – and for Cheng.

It was mid-morning and a picture-perfect day when they boarded the plane for Chicago. Ah, goodbye to Hawaii for now, but they all looked forward to a return visit on their way home!

The flight was long and tiring and they were greeted in Chicago with wind, dark clouds, and rain. The hotel was a welcomed sight, especially after a very fast ride with a "daredevil" cab driver. With the anticipation of comfortable beds and much needed rest before the start of their intense business schedule, they looked forward to the luxury of sleeping a little late tomorrow; their first meeting wasn't until 1:00.

Huan's eyes were still tired and his body achy the next morning, but his attention was quickly diverted to the fascinating American television – so many channels, movies, advertisements, and news stations! He could have stayed in his room all day with the remote control in his hand, just pushing the up and down arrows from one channel to another, but it was time for business. A light lunch, and they were out the door, back into the misty streets of Chicago. By late afternoon, the sky cleared and Chicago was much more appealing. This time they had the good fortune to team up with a cheery cab driver who was more than happy to show them the *real* Chicago. They loved it! Tall buildings, street dancers, a baseball field, beautiful parks and fountains dotted the route back to their hotel.

It was a busy week for the three businessmen from Beijing. They attended meetings, plant tours, product presentations, lunches, dinners, and even enjoyed live musical entertainment. They were delighted with the Chicago Cubs® baseball caps they received as souvenirs from one of their clients *and wore them a lot!*

Every morning they left the hotel with briefcases full of information about their company's services, and every evening they returned with American company portfolios, product specs, and business plans. And every night they methodically poured over the paperwork until they reached a consensus on how they would recommend proceeding...or not, in doing business with each company.

It was time to move on to Detroit, and Huan had not managed to free up any spare time to research the magazine article for Su-Li. There was no down time allotted for anything personal – it was all business. He came to the sad realization that he was probably going to return to China empty-handed with no useful information for his friend's family, and there was nothing he could do about it. He needed a couple of hours away from their meetings for a trip to the library or time to seek on-line help from someone with a computer, and that wasn't going to happen without a very good explanation! If it was just Li, there could be a chance for some time off, but he didn't know Xuegin very well. Xuegin was new to the Accounting Department, recently transferred from Finance. Huan knew he had to be cautious with Xuegin until his personal loyalties were known; all he knew about him was his company position.

Business in Detroit was not much different from business in Chicago except the meetings were fewer and longer with more intricate details to iron out. Finally, they had one day off that allowed for relaxation. It was Sunday...the library was closed.

Huan turned the television on and was amazed at all the church services being broadcasted...so many different religions and even some in other languages. He recognized Spanish and French. The phone rang. It was Li.

"Want to go to church this morning? I found a Catholic church a couple of blocks from here. Xuegin doesn't care to go, but I want to."

"Yes, so would I. What time?"

"How about meeting me in the lobby at 10:00? The clerk at the desk said it's within walking distance – only about ten minutes. That would give us plenty of time to get there for the 10:30 Mass."

Huan had never been in a Catholic church. "It is beautiful," he remarked to Li. They stayed after the service so they could admire the colorful stained-glass windows and examine the interesting statues. That was when Huan noticed something he didn't like.

"Li, do you suppose American Catholic churches are like our government churches?"

"In what way? Why do you ask?"

"There are cameras here. If this is not a government church, why does it have cameras?"

Their interest in the windows and statuary was noticed by an official church greeter who approached them and offered to answer any questions they might have before the next service started.

Both men had questions regarding the windows and other items inside the church, but Huan was still curious about the cameras.

"Why does your church have cameras?" he asked. "Does your government require them?"

At first their guide seemed puzzled by the question, but after realizing who her visitors were and why they might be asking, responded with knowledgeable information: "The cameras are for making a video of our 10:30 Mass each week. We use it for two purposes. First, it is shown on television a week later. If you look at your television schedule for 8:00 tonight, you can watch the service we had last week. Second, we mail copies to some of our members who are not physically able to come to church...people who are elderly, ill, or handicapped. In answer your question then, no, our government does not require them. It is just something we do for our congregation and anyone else who wants to see our services on television. Government in this country does not interfere with the Catholic Church, or with *any* church for that matter. We have freedom of religion and we also have separation of church and state."

Huan and Li were both confused.

"What is the difference between freedom of religion and separation of church and state?" Li asked.

"Freedom of religion is what you saw in our service today. We meet openly and as often as we wish. Our government does not tell us how to share the word of God. We share it many ways, but *how* we do it is our own choice.

"Separation of church and state means the government does not have a presence in the churches. Government does not tell churches or their members what to do or how to think. On the other hand, churches do not tell the government how to run the country. Churches are not allowed to put up religious pictures, statues, or signs in government buildings unless it would be considered a significant part of history, such as in a very old courthouse or library."

Li and Huan thanked the church greeter for her time and excellent information and walked back to the hotel.

"Thanks for inviting me to church, Li. I learned a lot about being Catholic and about religion in America. It was interesting."

Back on his own, Huan wandered through the hotel. There were quite a few people in the lobby and restaurants with computers, but Huan didn't feel comfortable asking a stranger for help with his quest for Su-Li's daughter. Besides, he had no idea how to log in even if he did find a willing person. He had access to only one computer in his life, and that was the one in his office which connected to the internet strictly for business purposes. Looking up information or contacting outside companies was done through a special channel by authorized personnel.

Sometimes he regretted not having a personal computer at home but, in all honesty, he enjoyed having peace and quiet on weekends without one. His fifteen-year-old son, Wei, definitely wanted one and asked several times for one, but Huan was not willing to let him poke around on the internet without guidance. "Someday," he told him... "but not yet."

It saddened Huan to have to tell his son "no," especially since it was a reasonable request from someone his age. But Wei was not the same child since Gong Li died. As hard as Huan tried to be both mother and father to their son, it was difficult; Wei was becoming a rebellious teenager with a less-than-desirable attitude. *No, he needs more time to mature before I can trust him with a computer,* Huan decided. *He needs to learn how to react to things he doesn't agree with in a non-confrontational manner. He needs to learn how to think more rationally. The internet might get him into trouble.*

Not having a computer and internet access at home wasn't going to help the situation he was in at the moment, however. He purchased a can of soda from a vending machine and strolled through the hotel shopping hall. The stores were closed, but it was still fun looking at the very expensive and luxurious things in the windows.

One place that *was* open on Sunday, however, was the hotel gift shop near the lobby. He wanted to buy something for Wei, who was undoubtedly enjoying the freedom of "being in charge of the house" for a couple of weeks, even though his aunt and uncle were keeping a close eye on him from next door.

A large assortment of model cars was the central window display. Appropriately, they were all cars made by Detroit companies. Surely Wei would enjoy one of these, but which one?

There were dozens to choose from. He stood in front of the window for quite a while before deciding to go in for a better look.

"May I help you with something?"

Huan turned around and shrugged at the blonde-haired young woman sitting behind the counter. "I am not from here – obviously," he said with a smile, "so I am not familiar with most of these automobiles. I want to take a gift back to my son in Beijing who is fifteen and developing a love for cars. What would you recommend?"

"Well, as a teenager," she offered as she made her way toward the window, "he would probably like a sports car or a muscle car. You might want to think about a Corvette or Camaro like these over here, or maybe something like this one," as she held up a Ford Mustang. "These are classic cars from the '60s and '70s, which I personally like better than the newer models. We have them in different colors, but there is not enough room in the window to display all of them. When you decide which one you like, I'll be happy to see what other colors we have in the back room."

"Actually, I like both of these," Huan replied as he examined the Corvette and the Mustang. "Maybe I should buy one of each, let my son choose the one he likes, and then his father can play with the other one!"

That brought a friendly laugh from the clerk. Ah, it felt good to be talking about something other than business!

"You sound just like my father, except he has a collection of the *real* cars as well. Let me take a look in back and see what colors I can find."

As the clerk disappeared behind a curtain, Huan glanced around the room and noticed an attractive piece of art work on the wall – a wooden carving of a piano, tilted kind of sideways. Wouldn't Su-Li love to have that, he thought. Then another idea came right in behind it!

Su-Li. Piano. Music lessons. Chinese children. Of course! That was how he could approach the subject with Li and Xuegin of looking up information on a computer! Somehow, he had to let them know that Cheng's wife is now a music teacher. She teaches piano and is looking for ways to help Chinese children grow in their musical ability. She is looking for opportunities to showcase Chinese music students to the rest of the world and has heard about groups of international students who come together and perform in different countries.

Yes! That is the course he could take! All he needed was the right timing – the right path of conversation.

"I have both models in three different colors," said the cheery sales clerk as she emerged from the curtains with six boxes in her hands. Which father and son colors appeal to you?"

"Definitely the red Mustang and the yellow Corvette. And I would like that wooden piano on the wall also. Can you wrap everything up really well? They've got a long way to travel!"

"The cars are already packaged with foam padding inside the boxes," she said, "and I will put lots of bubble wrap around the piano for you."

With two bags of gifts and a package of cookies, Huan headed for the elevator with a story coming together in his head. The light on his hotel phone was blinking as he walked into his room. Did he want to meet his companions down in the piano lounge for a meal so they could go over tomorrow's agenda? Yes, he did! Briefcase in hand, he walked back to the elevator.

The timing could not have been more perfect! Both elevators opened on the ground floor at the same time, allowing all three of the men to walk together toward the piano lounge. As they went past the gift shop, Huan waved to the clerk and she waved back.

"Enjoy your piano and cars!" she called out.

Huan savored the inquisitive looks from his companions.

"Pianos and cars?" Xuegin asked.

"Just one piano; two cars," he replied with a grin as he motioned them toward the window. "See this car over here, second one in from the left? It's a 1975 Chevrolet Corvette. I bought that one, only in yellow. The third car in the next row over is a 1968 Ford Mustang. I bought that one in red. One is for my son and the other one is for me. I'm pretty sure Wei will want the red one – at least I'm hoping he will because I like the yellow one better for myself."

Xuegin and Li, both being fathers and liking cars, understood completely. Huan waited, anticipating the next question as they continued down the hallway.

"And you bought a piano?"

Perfect, he thought – *and they brought the subject up themselves!* "Yes, for Su-Li. You remember Cheng's wife, Su-Li, don't you?"

Li remembered her, of course. Xuegin said he had never met her but...

...but knew I was going to meet with her a week ago about Cheng's dropped account, Huan said to himself as he silently finished Xuegin's sentence.

Huan knew the conversation was not going to end there; they would have more questions. But they were walking into the piano lounge. It would be a good opportunity for them to "scratch their heads" for a little while as they looked over the menu!

"While we have a few minutes, Huan, tell us about the piano you bought for Cheng's wife. I'm assuming it was a music box."

"No, not a music box – it's a wooden carving. It's kind of a strange story, actually. You know the ordeal we went through trying to figure out why we were still getting dividends on a stock that no one in our company owned and finally discovering it belonged to Cheng?"

The two men nodded as Huan continued. "If you will recall, I was supposed to contact Su-Li to find out what she wanted us to do about this remaining investment account. I had a hard time finding her at home until I finally had a chance to talk to one of her neighbors who told me Su-Li was working every day in another village. I went back to see her later on a weekend and finally caught her at home. Remember when Cheng died, we decided to give her his car as it was fully depreciated and wouldn't be worth much as a trade in?"

Yes, they remembered.

"Well, she decided to learn how to drive. The car didn't last long without requiring repairs, as we somewhat anticipated. But by that time, she was getting used to driving and bought herself another Volkswagen. So, because of our company's generosity in giving her Cheng's car and giving her an opportunity to drive, she was able to go to Beijing and be recertified as a teacher. She is now teaching music in another village and doing very well. As a result, she is thankful to our company.

"Her son, Qiang, who she includes when it comes to all financial decisions, was with us last week when we talked about Cheng's account and how it should be handled. Su-Li decided she wants the funds withdrawn and disbursed to her in a lump sum instead of an annuity. That came as a surprise to Qiang and me, as it probably is to you, as an annuity spread out over the long term would have been the choice for most people. Personally, an annuity is what I fully expected her to request, although she says she is doing very well on the income from Cheng's other accounts."

"Why did she request such a disbursement?" Li asked. "Did she explain why?"

"She wants to buy a piano. Her talented son refurbished a very old, damaged piano a few years ago for the school where she teaches. It was apparently in pretty rough shape, but Qiang was able to bring it back to usable condition so the children could use it to learn on. Unfortunately, it is starting to have problems again, but the children love it and love playing it. Su-Li decided that she wants to buy a new piano for her music class and donate it to the school in memory of Cheng. She said that the children in her music class are fascinated with the piano more than any of the other instruments and several of them are really very good at playing it, even such as it is.

"But there's more," Huan added as he moved aside for the waiter to deliver his scrumptious-looking hamburger and fries. He decided to enjoy a bite of his dinner before continuing, noting that his co-workers were doing the same although obviously waiting to hear the rest of his story.

He continued: "Apparently Su-Li learned of a group of international students, probably university students, who have been given a chance to perform with symphonies in different countries. She is trying to find out more information so her best students can have a goal of representing China someday as part of such a group. She said she has not had time to travel to Beijing to visit the music department at the university to do research, so I got the impression that she has not shared her idea with anyone in authority yet. She does not have a computer at home, so that is probably why she has to go to Beijing.

"I am very impressed with Su-Li's good intentions and the dream she has for Chinese children. When I saw the wooden carving of a piano in the gift shop, I decided to buy it for her. It was just an impulsive purchase. I wish I could do more for her, especially since Cheng was my good friend, but I know very little about searching for information on a computer except what we do in our company, and I know even less about music."

The rest of the dinner conversation was devoted to the next day's schedule, concluding earlier than expected. They agreed to get to bed early and be ready to tackle the next day with lots of vigor as they wrapped up their business in Detroit. The fact that several people around them were working on computers while they ate, plugged into special outlets right at the tables, was not lost on any of them, especially Li.

"Hey, Huan, "I saw a row of booths in the hallway next to the lobby where people are using hotel computers. Why don't we see if we can find some information for Su-Li? I'm sure we can get someone to help us if we can't figure it out. How different can it be from our company computers?"

Perfect again, Huan thought with straight-faced amusement. *Someday I will have to thank Li for walking straight into my plan!*

"You're right, Li," said Xuegin. "How different can it be? And won't Cheng's wife be surprised if we come home with some helpful information. Why don't we give it a try?"

It was *very* different! After several failed attempts to give the computer whatever information it needed to connect to the internet, they decided in the best interest of time to ask the desk clerk for help. It didn't take the clerk long to recognize their lack of computer savvy and politely suggested that they come back in a half hour when his supervisor would be returning from dinner. Perhaps he could help them.

That changed everything. Li and Xuegin lost their enthusiasm for Su-Li's cause and decided they didn't want to be up late learning about the idiosyncrasies of a computer system when they could be watching television or sleeping.

"Well, maybe I will come back down and maybe I won't," Huan commented casually, inwardly relieved that he was just handed a perfect opportunity to find the information he sought in private. "I'll see you tomorrow. 8:00 right here."

He spent most of the next half hour meticulously writing down the information he wanted, followed by a list of suggested key words to aid in the search. He at least knew that much about the internet! He wrote down the most important words first, and waited for his "tutor."

Matt was a middle-aged, slightly plump, pleasant man, more than willing to help a hotel guest. Huan apologized for his lack of knowledge with American computers, but when Matt saw that Huan had a key word list already compiled, he offered to do the search for him while he waited. Matt's fingers tapped away at keys faster than Huan's eyes could follow, with pictures and messages popping up and disappearing on the screen. After ten minutes of Huan answering yes or no to each site he pulled up, Matt proudly handed Huan printouts of exactly what he was looking for...date and place of the concert, names of the guest musicians, program of song selections, and a promotional paragraph about the student group. The young woman's name was Emily Thornton from London, Ontario, Canada.

"Do you want to know where the group is performing this year," asked Matt?

"Yes. Can you find that information for me?"

"Sure can. There's a link here for their 2003 schedule plus the first half of next year's as well. There's another link for bio information on each of the students, too, if you want it."

"Just the one for Emily."

The bio sheet included an enlarged formal picture of Emily; her hair was *exactly* like Su-Li's.

"Here's another group picture. It's not an action shot of them playing, but it's a nice picture. Want me to print it out for you?"

Huan looked away from the schedule he held in his hand and back at the screen. Emily was smiling in this picture...and it was like he was looking at Cheng. Emily *had* to be Cheng's daughter – she had his exact smile! There was no doubt in his mind he was looking at a picture of Xiu-Su!

"Please. That picture will be very helpful."

The printer cranked out the last page and Huan added it to his stack. "Thank you very much for all of your help, Matt. How much do I owe you?"

"Absolutely nothing; we're always happy to help our guests. I'm just pleased we were able to find what you were looking for. Have a good evening, sir."

Huan hurried back to his room to study his cache of treasures, trying to imagine how Su-Li and Qiang were going to handle such definitive information. How will they react? What will they do next – what *could* they do? Well, one thing at a time, he decided. First, he had to get this stuff to them without Li and Xuegin seeing it. He sat down with pen and paper and wrote out bits and pieces of generic information that he could show them if they asked.

Sleep did not come easy. Meeting Li and Xuegin the next morning in the lobby, he said: "You were right. I should have gone to bed earlier instead of spending time with that computer, although I did find a little information that might be useful to Su-Li. Well, maybe. At least it will be a start if she wishes to pursue it further."

"Did you learn anything useful about computer technology?" Xuegin asked with an amused grin.

"Yes. I learned that I don't want to know anything more about computers than necessary to do my job."

Both men smiled and nodded their heads in understanding. A few minutes later, and they were out the door to a waiting cab.

###

With their last day of meetings in Detroit wrapped up, it was time to embark on the third and final leg of their intense business trip that would take them to Toronto, Ontario, Canada. Li had a map of Ontario and showed them where Toronto was. "It will be a short flight, not much longer than the one from Chicago to Detroit," he told them. Huan also noticed that London, Ontario, Canada – the home of Emily's family, was not far from Toronto.

Getting through Customs was a slow process for three Chinese citizens flying from the United States into Canada. All of their belongings were searched, including Huan's model cars, piano carving, and folders of business papers. He held his breath as a customs official leafed through a stack of business papers, among which he had interspersed the printouts from Matt. Thankfully, Li and Xuegin were busily engaged in putting their own suitcases and briefcases back in order.

"You're all set, gentlemen; here are your boarding passes. Have a good flight."

What a different country Canada was from the United States! It was strange, they decided, how two large countries joined together could be so different – different money, signs, mileage markers, measurements of fuel, food, and the way they talked. It was English, but a slightly different English than the one they learned in Beijing.

Their Canadian hosts were delightful; the meetings pleasant and productive. Another plus was that downtown Toronto was very accessible, especially after they discovered the unique underground tunnel system that connected their hotel with shopping areas and even the airport. Yes, they were pleased with their new Canadian contacts and were sure their management would be also.

It was finally time to say good-bye to the business world of North America and head for their return stop-over: the beaches of Hawaii. The warm sand and sunshine were inviting as they wound down and adjusted once again to time zone changes.

Next stop: Beijing and home! Huan was anxious to get back to Su-Li and her family to show them what he found. Success in uncovering information about Xiu-Su was important to him for another reason as well. It was the first instance he knew of where there was a possibility of reuniting a family. He would present Su-Li with the piano first, he decided, and then then lay out the paperwork in the most meaningful order, saving the picture for last. Doing so would also be a sense of closure for him – to finally be able to say thank you to Cheng, in a strange way, for all of the help he gave him and Gong Li. But in the back of his mind, he still struggled with thoughts of that day five years ago when fate placed him up on the deck of the ship instead of on the dock. It could just as easily have been him standing on the dock instead of Cheng or Yao.

Why did it happen that way? Why was he spared?

No sooner had those haunting thoughts entered his mind *once again,* than the answer became as clear as the blue sky outside the window of his plane!

If Cheng had not died, he suddenly realized, *Su-Li would not have learned to drive; she would have had no reason to. She never would have been in the car dealership to find the picture of Xiu-Su in a travel magazine. She never would have discovered the picture of her daughter or ever had any hope of finding her! It was God's timing! It had to be!*

It was the next Tuesday when Huan was finally able to meet with Su-Li, Qiang, and Guo. He felt almost shy as he handed Su-Li the brightly colored package with the piano. In keeping with Chinese tradition when receiving a gift, she set it aside to open later.

"Please open it now, Su-Li," Huan coaxed. It is part of the story that I want to tell you."

She marveled at the beauty of the gift, but even more so at the handsomely inscribed wooden plaque Huan had made to be placed on the wall underneath:

Share the Music of Chinese Children with the World

He hadn't intended to make her tear up, though he knew they were happy tears. Proper tradition was important to Su-Li, of course, but Huan was destined to see a side of his hostess experienced by very few. Instead of the customary smile and nod upon receiving a gift, he received a surprising hug from Cheng's lovely lady!

It was time! One by one, he pulled the papers out of his briefcase, starting with a printed enlargement of the picture and article from the travel magazine. Then the next printout, and the next, giving them time to absorb each one.

Two of the final three pages – the bio of Emily with her close-up personal picture, and the casual group picture with a smiling Emily leaning on the piano, put their excitement over the top. There was no doubt in anyone's mind that Emily *had* to be Xiu-Su! Her face and hair was Su-Li; her smile was Cheng. As they continued to study the array of information laid out before them, the room turned silent. Su-Li looked over at Huan.

"My friend, never could anyone ever, ever give me a better gift...except for the day I learned that she had not died." She looked over at Qiang and smiled.

"I have wondered for twenty years what my daughter would look like, trying to picture her face at different ages. When I found out she was alive, then I wondered where she was living and what she was doing with her life. Now I know. Even if I never get to see her...now I know."

It was a bittersweet moment: the joy of finding a lost child, tempered with the reality that she was still out of reach. Su-Li instinctively turned toward Qiang and buried her face in his shirt until she could compose herself and turn back to her guest.

When he felt everything was settled back down, Huan handed them the last document – the group's schedule of upcoming appearances for the last half of 2003 and the first part of 2004. One date was circled. The group of international music students was scheduled to play in Beijing in the spring of 2004 – just months away!

They looked at the schedule in astonishment, then looked at each other – and finally back at Huan. Where was this leading? Was he thinking that possibly…?

"We *might* be able to make this happen," he said quietly, affirming their anticipation. "At least I think my company can. I 'kind of' contorted the reason I was buying the piano for you to my two co-workers."

He looked over with a mischievous grin at their still confused faces. "While we were on our business trip, I informed them of your desire to purchase a piano with funds from Cheng's account, Su-Li, and donate it to your music class in his memory. I also made known to them your strong goal as a music teacher to elevate some of your students to someday represent China in such a group as the one we had discussed. They thought that these were noble things for you to want to do and were agreeable that I should take the time to find information for you, if possible, on a hotel computer.

"Therefore, when I bring the subject up again, they will remember that I found some useful information for you, although we didn't discuss *what* I found. And when I can show them an example of such a group of students coming to Beijing, I feel they would be supportive in suggesting to our management that we arrange to purchase tickets for you. It would be good for our company to support the local symphony and, at the same time, do something thoughtful for the family of an employee who was held in high esteem. I cannot promise, but I will try my best to obtain three tickets for the Beijing concert."

The quest was over, successful, and the results were laid out before his friends. It was time to leave and allow them privacy to ponder their new information. Huan promised to let them know of his success – or lack of, with obtaining tickets.

As he drove back to Beijing, his mind was preoccupied with the emotions of the evening and the exciting possibility of a family reunited. He never saw the speeding truck coming around a curve and crossing over the center of the road until it was too late. It hit him head on. The last thing he remembered was his car skidding off the side of the road, a hard bump, being airborne and landing upside down.

Li and Xuegin could not believe the news awaiting them when they arrived at the office Wednesday morning. Huan had been in an accident and was in the hospital in critical condition! He had a concussion, spinal trauma, broken bones, and lacerations. Company personnel were seeing to his needs and those of his son, Wei. They were handed the briefcase retrieved from Huan's car with instructions to go through it and identify anything that might need attention.

This was the day they were scheduled to make their official report to management, with Huan being the leader of the presentation. They asked for and received a day's postponement so they could look over Huan's notes and be prepared. They pulled everything out of the briefcase. The presentation was neatly arranged in its own folder, with duplicate copies collated, stapled, and ready to be handed out. There were several folders of other projects Huan was working on, but nothing urgent as far as they could determine. The last folder was personal papers – bills, receipts, his expense report, a few reminder notes. Maybe Huan would be able to have visitors in a few days and they could ask him how they should take care of any personal things that needed to be done.

Li pulled out one more paper from Huan's personal folder – some kind of schedule of performances for a group of students. It puzzled them at first. Was his son taking music lessons? Then Li remembered what Huan had said about finding a little information for Su-Li and something about opportunities for Chinese music students to perform in other countries.

"This is probably what Huan was doing," said Li. "He must have been coming back from showing this to Cheng's wife. Remember what he said? He said that he found a little information, not much, but it would at least be a start for her."

He noticed the one date that was circled. "Look, Xuegin. This group is going to be in Beijing in a few months. My guess is that Huan was probably showing this to Su-Li in case she wanted to pursue it." He started to put it back into the briefcase.

"Wait a minute, Li. I wonder if he was going to try to get tickets for her. Why else would he have this with him instead of leaving it with her? Offering to obtain tickets for a concert right here in

Beijing would seem a logical thing to do, especially for Huan. If that is the case, maybe we should put it with the other things we want to ask him about. He might want us to follow through on it for him. Of course, we could just ask Su-Li. We should probably go to see her anyway and tell her about Huan. They are apparently good friends; I'm sure she would want to know. Well, hopefully he will improve soon and we can talk to him."

"I agree, Xuegin, but I think it would be helpful if we could talk with Huan *before* we visit Su-Li. Then we can give her a better account first hand of his condition. Right now, however, let's get through this presentation tomorrow so we can start implementing our new customer channels."

Huan understood everything his brother and sister-in-law and Wei said, but communication was one way. His vocal cords were not working; his throat hurt...a lot! He could manage slight facial expressions, but couldn't move his head or neck. Wherever he moved his eyes he could see the edges of what seemed to be a large metal restrainer keeping his head and neck immobile. Other than the discomfort from whatever was on his head, the rest of his body had no feeling; he couldn't make anything move. He responded to questions by blinking his eyes once for yes and twice for no, but it was tiring. He just wanted to keep his eyes closed and rest.

Inwardly, however, he was thinking about his son. Almost overnight it seemed that Wei was somehow transformed from an irresponsible teenager to an adult as he insisted on taking charge of his father's care. Huan knew how much Wei missed his mother, but didn't realize how much his son loved him as well. It wasn't exactly something that fathers and sons talk about, he acknowledged silently, but knowing that Wei didn't want to leave his bedside said a lot. *Maybe something good can come from this after all*, he thought.

As sad as his condition was, a spark of reality told him that maybe it was time for Wei to have a computer. If he was mature enough to take care of an incapacitated father and manage the house by himself, he should be able to deal judiciously with the internet!

Huan woke up several nights later because his foot was twitching or cramping – or doing something! Whatever it was, it created a stir on the machine that was monitoring his body. Within minutes a nurse and doctor were in his room, poking at his foot and leg, bending his fingers. The inflammation from spinal trauma was subsiding, he was told. Yes! Even though it hurt, it felt good at the same time; he was getting some feeling back! He could even whisper a little – it was going to be a good day!

The visit from Li and Xuegin was another bright spot in his day. After hearing about how well the presentation to management went, they spent a short time going over Huan's other project folders, receiving whispered instructions on what could wait and what should be handled by someone else.

"One last thing, Huan, and then we will let you rest for a while. We were told our visit was limited to fifteen minutes so we have to make it quick."

Li pulled the music students' schedule from a folder and held it up so he could see it. Huan felt a chill when he recognized what it was – an extra copy to remind him about getting tickets.

"We found this in your briefcase and guessed you were probably driving back home from Su-Li's house when you had your accident as you were coming from that direction. We figured you might have gone there to deliver whatever information you found for her in Detroit. Right?"

His throat was getting sore, but he cautiously whispered "yes," not knowing where the conversation was heading.

"There's a Beijing performance circled. Were you going to try to get tickets for her by any chance?"

Another "yes." But why would they think that, he wondered?

"You are such a nice guy, Huan! Xuegin chided. "Do you want us to follow through on this for you?"

"Yes."

"How many?"

"Three."

"We thought that's what this paper was all about so I went ahead and inquired about tickets. They won't go on sale for another month. I put the date on my calendar so I won't forget to call because apparently these concert performances get sold out quickly. If you agree, we will go to Su-Li tomorrow to let her know of your accident. Li says he remembers how to get there. We just wanted to wait until we were allowed to visit you first and give her an account of your condition. Do you want us to tell her that we are going to try to get tickets or do you want that surprise to wait until you can tell her yourself?"

"Let her know."

"We also had another great idea," Li chimed in proudly. "We thought that our management might be receptive to purchasing the tickets as a gift from our company, and perhaps arranging for Su-Li and her family to personally meet with the group of students after the concert if it is allowed. It might be good public relations for our company to officially sponsor Su-Li in her endeavor to promote her music students and China in the future with a group such as this. What do you think? Personally, we think it is a brilliant idea!"

If they only knew, thought Huan!

"Brilliant!" he whispered with as much of a smile as he could muster with his swollen face. "Absolutely brilliant!"

Su-Li was gradually settling down from the excitement of all the information about Xiu-Su, or Emily as she had to get used to calling her, plus *the possibility* of actually being able to see her daughter and hear her play the piano. She was anticipating news from Huan to let her know if he was able to get tickets to the concert. Other than that, she was looking forward to a quiet Sunday evening as she prepared her lessons for the week. When the two men came to her door, she vaguely remembered Li as being from Cheng's company. *More about Cheng's mysterious account,* she thought.

"Good evening, Su-Li. Do you remember me? I am Li Ju. I was one of the men who brought you the sad news about Cheng. The last time I saw you was at your husband's funeral service. This is Xuegin Wong, who works in the Accounting Department."

Why would they introduce themselves in such a manner, she wondered? *Why were they referring to Cheng's funeral instead of a change in the account or more paperwork? Where is Huan?* "Yes, of course I remember you and your kindness, Li. Please come in. May I fix you both some tea?"

"Yes, that would be most gracious."

As Su-Li prepared a fresh pot of tea, Xuegin poked Li and pointed to the carved piano art piece on the wall. "I see Huan has been here, Su-Li. We helped him get that piano all the way back here in one piece from the United States by way of Canada."

"Yes," she smiled, returning from the kitchen with the tea tray. "I don't know which is more special – the piano or the message underneath."

They walked over to examine it. "Ah, Huan! Forever the sentimentalist," Li chuckled. "Actually, I would be more correct to say that is 'typically' Huan – always doing something nice for someone. That's just the way he is, and that is one of the reasons we are here."

Good! "Doing something nice" sounded better than "we are sorry to inform you!"

"We won't take up a lot of your time, Su-Li, but first, we are here once again with sad news. Tuesday night, after coming to visit you, our friend Huan was in a serious automobile accident and...."

Her heart sank! A shiver of de je vu swept over her as she remembered the night he came to tell her about Cheng. "Oh, no! Please tell me he is alright!"

"He has serious injuries," Li explained, "but is steadily recuperating. There are problems with his spine and neck and he cannot speak, only whisper. There will be a lot of therapy needed as the swelling goes down and his broken bones heal, but the outlook gets better each day."

Spine. Neck. Can't speak. Broken bones. Oh, no! Huan! She could feel tears ready to spill down her cheeks.

Li quickly added: "But the doctors are anticipating complete recovery, Su-Li. He is in good spirits. We are all keeping positive thoughts and I didn't mean to alarm you. Huan would not be happy with us if we caused you to cry!"

"I'm sorry. It's just that Huan has been such a dear friend and so helpful to Qiang and me since Cheng died. He is a special person."

"Well, Xuegin and I were given Huan's briefcase the day after his accident so we could take care of his paperwork, and among his papers was this performance schedule." He handed the paper to Su-Li.

Distrust of these two men immediately crept into her mind as she held Emily's schedule in her hand. *What do they know? How much do they know?* She squelched her fear, consciously forcing her hand to be steady and not shake, and looked up at Li with the most expressionless face she could manage.

"We know through Huan of the wonderful goal you have of promoting some of your star music students to be showcased through groups such as this. He told us of your idea while we were traveling after we asked why he was buying that piece of piano art. He obviously was so impressed with what you want to do that he spent part of the night finding information for you on a hotel computer rather than sleeping."

Whew. Relief rushed back in as she accepted the smiles of her visitors.

"When we saw this schedule," Li continued, "we assumed that he had shared such information with you. He also had this date circled which we interpreted to mean that he might have been trying to find a way for you to attend the Beijing concert."

"Yes, that is correct. He was here Tuesday evening and gave me the information you have there."

"That's what we thought as we tried to piece everything together that was in his briefcase. When we spoke with Huan a few days later, he confirmed our thoughts as best he could. Our management has asked us, therefore, to obtain tickets for you and your son and daughter-in-law if indeed you would like to attend the concert."

God is wonderful! God is wonderful! Those words echoed in Su-Li's head as she realized the door that just opened up for her...except she felt deeply saddened for Huan, her wonderful friend. "We would absolutely love to attend the concert, Li, if you could arrange for tickets. I am very interested in possibilities such as this for my students, plus Qiang and I both love piano. I play and teach piano and Qiang restores them. My new daughter-in-law, Guo, is learning ways to help Qiang with his restoration business and enjoys listening. She is also learning to be a tuner. Such an opportunity would be very special for all of us...and we would be happy to pay for them, of course."

"That is not necessary, Su-Li. It is a gift from our company. We will purchase them in the name of our company, if you have no objection, as we are pleased to be able to promote such a worthy cause as you represent. You are to be admired for your work with the children. I hope you don't mind having our company sponsor you in this endeavor."

"I would be honored to represent your company as well as my school and students. Your company was kind to Cheng and is continuing to be kind to me. Thank you, and please offer my appreciation to your management and to both of you as well for recognizing Huan's good intentions. And please, please, let me know as soon as we can visit him."

"He is allowed to have a few visitors now, but only company representatives and family, and for just fifteen minutes at a time. It will probably be a week or two until he gets a little more strength. I know he will welcome your visit eventually, but right now he has to remain quiet so broken bones can heal before he starts therapy. Plus, surgery to fuse his spine is still a possibility; it will depend on how much feeling comes back by itself. He is starting to have tingling in his feet and fingers, so we are hoping that he will not need surgery."

"Oh, how I wish this horrible thing had not happened to him! Please tell him we will see him as soon as we are allowed to visit. I am so saddened by this news, but am thankful his outlook is good."

"We will be seeing him tomorrow and will give him your message. Good day, Su-Li."

Once again Su-Li wished she had a telephone so she could call Qiang and Guo. Getting one was on top of the list of things to do this Tuesday when they made their weekly visit. The news about Huan would have to wait until then. *If only...If only Huan had not been here last week, this would not have happened! No, that is not right*, she reminded herself. *We don't control destiny. God does.*

###

Qiang and Guo took the "good news/bad news" just as Su-Li had, although Guo was especially saddened. The good friend and faithful worker that she knew since her teenage years was seriously hurt. She would let her family know, as well as all the others involved with the children's cause in Beijing, so they could quietly monitor his progress.

The calendar date was circled – nineteen weeks until they might be able to see Xiu-Su in person…no, her name was now Emily! Would they be able to get close enough to talk to her? How would they handle such a casual meeting? What would they say when they met her? They were filled with nervous anticipation.

"We have to remember that this is not about us, Mother," said Qiang. "We will be representing your school, the students in your music class, and Father's company. Whatever happens over and above that will not be up to us. God has brought us this far, so what happens will be up to Him. We are just walking the path He has set before us. We have to think and conduct ourselves with alert minds, not our hearts. We have to be careful."

As always, Qiang was the one with clear thinking. Yes, emotion had to be kept to a minimum, they all agreed. But in her heart, Su-Li longed for the moment she could look into her daughter's eyes once again – hopefully up close.

SHOES IN THE RIVER

Chapter 12: Love Changes Everything

2003 – 2004

It was their third trip to visit Huan in the hospital. The first one was the worst. Even though Su-Li, Qiang, and Guo knew the extent of his injuries, it was still a shock to see a man who was so healthy the last time they saw him now propped up in bed with a sling to keep pressure from his spine and a large metal loop encompassing the top of his head. His left arm from shoulder to hand was in a cast, and broken ribs were healing inside his bandaged torso. But after they got past the appearance, they couldn't help but be heartened by his upbeat attitude. He was thankful that feeling was coming back into his legs and he was able to stand and take a few steps. He could speak slightly above the whisper he had been limited to for weeks.

There was a definite improvement on the second visit over the first, and Guo was excited to be able to tell her family and friends the good news: Huan was not going to need spinal surgery! The metal ring on his head was replaced with a plastic collar, all of his stitches and clamps were removed, and there were fewer tubes attached to his body. Good news, good news, and more good news!

Today's visit was going to be different, however. Qiang was in school and Guo had a job interview. Su-Li was visiting Huan without them, but not alone – Wu Liang and her son Shing were with her.

It was through Qiang that Wu learned of Huan's accident. He casually told Wu about his mother's good news of an unexpected income, her choice to purchase a piano for her students in Cheng's memory, and finally mentioning the accident his father's friend and co-worker was involved in after his last visit.

"Oh no! Not Huan Qu'nan!" she said to a surprised Qiang. "Huan and his wife were good friends of mine when I lived in Beijing. Gong Li and I knew each other from school. I remember when she first met Huan and told me how nice he was – always upbeat and smiling. Gong Li was the same way...they were such a perfect couple! I lost touch with them after Guang died because I didn't travel to Beijing much anymore. I had no reason to go back there except to occasionally bring pieces of art to his store contacts. In fact, I never heard about Gong Li dying until a year after she was gone. Oh, I have been so out of touch with the group in Beijing! And now Huan! Would it be alright if I visited him? Are children allowed? Can Shing come with me? Huan will probably remember Shing."

Huan knows so many people, Qiang reminded himself. *First Guo, now Wu. I should not be surprised! Not only is he a businessman who travels all over China just like Father did, especially in Beijing, he and his wife were involved with the children's cause in Beijing for years.*

"No visitors yet, Wu, but I will let you know when that changes. I'll ask if children are allowed. I am sure Huan will be surprised and happy to see you."

###

Today was the day they were going to surprise Huan, but Su-Li was just as excited about seeing him as Wu was – she wanted to thank him for the tickets Xuegin brought to Qiang's apartment two nights ago.

The call from Qiang about the tickets was the first official call she received on her new phone. She had three so far: one from Qiang and another from Guo as test calls, and finally a "real" call with this exciting news. Now the count-down of days until she saw Xiu-Su held a definite conclusion, not just a hope. A telephone was such an exciting addition to her life – almost as much as learning to drive and owning a car! What was next? She was thinking about a computer.

Wei was sitting at the side of his father's bed when they arrived, gently massaging feeling back into Huan's recently unwrapped, pale arm. No more cast! They looked puzzled when a strange woman and child walked into the room with Su-Li, but as soon as Wu spoke, Huan realized who she was. His face lit up! He had not seen Wu in years, nor Shing since he was a small child. Shing didn't remember, of course, but took an *instant* liking to Wei. For the rest of their visit, young Shing was no more than a couple of feet from Wei's elbow...and Wei didn't seem to mind at all!

After telling Huan about the tickets and how much they were appreciated, Su-Li found a magazine and comfortable chair in the corner and decided to let the two old friends enjoy each other's company and reminiscing. She looked up a couple of times and noticed that Huan seemed very attentive to Wu.

Suddenly it occurred to her...Huan was not just attentive. He looked happy; he was smiling and truly enjoying Wu's company! Was it her imagination or was there perhaps a spark igniting between them? *What a wonderful couple they would make,* she thought!

"Wei and Shing, would you like to go to the lunch room with me for some ice cream? I'm not sure if I remember exactly how to get there. My throat is dry and ice cream sure would taste good. Maybe we could even bring some back for *your parents* if we walk fast enough so it doesn't melt."

"Your parents" wasn't meant to be a premonition, but it was.

A whole new relationship evolved for Huan and Wu. It was a rekindled friendship that Huan realized most likely would not have happened if it hadn't been for his near fatal accident. Again, he thought about the sudden revelation he experienced the day he was flying back home from his business trip: if Cheng hadn't died, Su-Li never would have found her daughter. *Sometimes drastic things are just meant to be so other things can happen,* he told himself, a*nd finding Wu again was definitely meant to be!* It had been a long time since he felt this happy.

Wu and Shing made trips to the hospital and rehab center every few days to be with Huan. Wu became his unofficial caregiver and coach if Wei wasn't there. But if Wei wasn't there, Shing's whole day was ruined! The two boys were four years apart in age, but soon became inseparable – as did Huan and Wu.

When Huan was finally released to go home, all that remained from the accident were scars and a dull pain in his lower back when the weather changed. It was a day for celebration – and another surprise. He found the house unbelievably clean and orderly. Wei had definitely turned a corner!

Changes were in the air for Huan and Wu! There were many decisions to be made, and the one to get married was the easiest.

They had a small wedding in Huan's Christian church in Beijing. As much as they both loved their spouses who died, it was time to stop living in the past. That was what the preacher told them...remember and appreciate your former life, but don't let it cast a shadow over your future. Let it go. As they stepped onto the path that led to a new life together, they also had something that many couples in China did not have: *two children!* – two children who knew what it was like not to have a sibling, and then the joy of change! The boys were as close as two brothers could possibly be.

Other decisions were not as easy. Huan and Wu knew Beijing was where they would live because of Huan's job, but what about Wu's building and her studio? Should she sell it or keep it and rent to tenants?

Shortly after Huan returned to work, he was offered a different position at his company with more responsibilities – one that would oversee both the Operations *and* Finance Departments. That would mean international travel. Should he accept it? Would Wu be comfortable having him out of the country from time to time?

And what about Mulan? She had always been faithful to Wu and Shing. Now that Shing had additional grandparents, would Mulan feel less important or lonely with her only grandson being farther away? How would Shing feel about not seeing Mulan as often? After all, he spent a lot of time with her while growing up, especially during those times when his mother was setting up her business or was out of town. Then there was Wu's promise to Mulan after Guang died that she would always help and support her. It was Chinese custom and her responsibility as a daughter-in-law.

So many questions; so many decisions, but Huan made it easier. "Worrying doesn't help, Wu. Trust me," he said with a smile. "We can worry about all kinds of problems, real or perceived, but it will be the unexpected things in our lives that will test our strength and shape our future. I have learned that first-hand."

How Huan sounded so much like Guang, she thought for just a moment. How could she have been so fortunate...no, blessed, to have two such dear men in her life? "You are right, Huan. Let's get our own lives and house in order first...one thing at a time. We should be more like our children, who don't seem to have a care in the world. Whatever we decide to do will undoubtedly be fine with them. Meanwhile, we have two houses to look at tomorrow morning while the boys are in school."

Life was good for Huan and Wu Qu'nan and sons.

With all of their family gone from the village, Su-Li and Mulan decided they were not going to be "wimpy women who could not make their own decisions!" Ever since Qiang married and moved to Beijing, the sunshine in Su-Li's personal life dimmed. When Wu married and moved away, taking Shing with her, Mulan was also depressed. The two women drew closer together as they commiserated over their distant families.

But today was different. This was the day they were going to get out of their slump and, in Mulan's words, "pull ourselves up by our boot straps and take charge of our future." Su-Li started their moving ahead session by quoting words from her former missionary teacher, Roberto:

"Life goes on, even as the world changes. We also must be willing to change."

There was one thing they both already decided – it was time to sell their houses and move to apartments in or near Beijing. Today was the day they were going to discuss options, map out plans, and set their time frame. It was a fruitful session as the two women set the wheels in motion. They just did it their own way – with a big plate of honey cakes and a large pot of tea.

Su-Li's time frame was already sealed. She was scheduled to start her new job in Beijing in three months, thanks to Professor Zi.

As much as Hua Zi was reluctant to lose Su-Li as a teacher, it was to his credit that he offered her as a candidate for a new position in Beijing at a school of higher learning. The Administrator of Schools in Beijing was looking for someone with not just good academic qualifications, but with energy and commitment for a recently created position. It was working with teenage students who showed superior musical promise –like the ones coming to the symphony hall in several weeks.

Su-Li's resume' was impressive, especially with Hua Zi's letter of recommendation. It mentioned her personal commitment to reviving their derailed music program and to restoring their "hopeless" piano and long-neglected instruments. It also included appreciation for the new piano donated to the school in honor of her deceased husband.

"These are things that go far above normal expectations," his letter concluded. "Su-Li is more than a teacher. She is genuinely committed to her cause of promoting her students and the children of China to more serious participation in the global world of traditional and classical music. Her young students have already performed in churches, at weddings, and in local concerts. Teacher Ming is currently being sponsored in her efforts by her deceased husband's company which is based in Beijing. She is worthy of an interview."

The invitation to interview took Su-Li completely by surprise, as did the letter a month later with a formal job offer – which she accepted. It all happened so fast! Her starting salary was almost twice that of her current position at Professor Zi's school. Because the job in Beijing was new, there was no training involved – just a tour of the building, location of her classroom, list of students, inventory of musical instruments, a budget, and goals.

Mulan was already thinking about moving to Beijing, even before Wu announced her marriage. She knew Beijing was a good market for Wu's art work; she traveled there a lot. Mulan anticipated that Wu and Shing would eventually move to Beijing – it just seemed logical. Now with Su-Li's acceptance of a new job, procrastination ended. There was nothing left to tie Mulan to the village she lived in since she was first married; no one there needed her any more. She took the first step...she signed up for driving lessons.

Chapter 13: Emily

2004 and Beyond

Why does every trip to Beijing have to be filled with the jitters? Qiang has the symphony tickets, Guo has opera glasses, and I have a stomach full of butterflies!

Just "getting there" felt like an eternity to Su-Li as she bounced along in her car. Well, maybe she wasn't bouncing – maybe it was more like squirming. The road was smooth, so it must be her. Tomorrow night she would see Xiu-Su!

She turned into the apartment complex where her son and daughter-in-law lived and lifted her suitcase from the passenger seat. It was going to be a short visit to attend the concert and return home. Then she and Mulan were planning to come back to Beijing a week later to look at apartments. Even though she would miss her village when the house she lived in for twenty-nine years sold, she would not miss the long drive between the village and Beijing. Mulan shared her sentiments. The move was going to happen and *everyone* was excited – Qiang, Guo, Huan, Wu, and Shing. Wei was too busy with school and a new brother to be concerned about who lived where. He was just happy if his little brother was happy.

"Mother! Let me take that suitcase for you. Qiang will be home soon. He had an exam today and I know he will be glad to get it behind him so he can enjoy the symphony tomorrow. We are so excited about Emily and finding out for sure if she really is Xiu-Su. I'm not sure how we will know except for the hair. I am probably just as nervous as you both are......"

It made Su-Li laugh to hear Guo vent her anxiety with run-on rambling sentences; she knew exactly how her daughter-in-law felt!

Guo found the symphony web site on-line and noticed that the conductor was going to hold a "meet the musicians" question and answer session for a half hour before the concert. Hoping that the guest musicians would be included, Su-Li, Qiang, and Guo arrived early.

Being back in the symphony hall felt strangely comforting for Su-Li, eliciting memories from many years ago. She and Cheng attended concerts there as university students. While the aura of the building felt familiar, the décor was much more ornate than she remembered. The lobby seemed bigger; the walls more colorful. There were beautiful lights, plush carpeting, and lounge chairs.

While Qiang was parking the car and Guo was inquiring about the location of the conductor's meeting, Su-Li walked over to the large, glass-covered poster just inside the entrance. It was similar to the picture she had from the travel magazine – just a different symphony and conductor. Off to one side was the same picture of the visiting music students, only much larger. There was Emily with her hands on the piano.

Looking at the poster suddenly filled Su-Li with a new and overwhelming sensation – the pride of a parent for a performing child! It was a whole different level of excitement from the auditorium where she and Cheng attended Qiang's school performances. They were always proud of him, of course, but this...was not a school. It was a symphony hall. The people walking by were not parents, teachers, and fellow classmates. They were strangers who came to be entertained with professional music. And that beautiful face before her was most likely her very own daughter!

But the feeling was fleeting as she pulled her thoughts back to Qiang's words of months ago. They had to be careful. They were not the family of a performing artist tonight. They were just members of the audience. The only thing special was that Su-Li was representing her husband's company. Anything more than that was out of their hands.

Soon Qiang and Guo were at her side, also anxiously studying the enlarged picture of Emily. Then, conscientiously putting their excitement aside, they made their way down the hall toward the conductor's meeting. Guo went on ahead and found the room, motioning for Qiang and Su-Li to follow. "Shall we?" Qiang said with a mischievous smile as he offered his arm to his mother.

"Yes, we shall, my handsome son," she grinned right back. "Let's go in and perhaps meet someone special!"

When the maestro's reception was concluded, however, the students had not yet arrived. They were stalled in traffic and a police escort was on its way to guide them to the music hall. They would be arriving in a few minutes...but it was time to be seated.

Xuegin did an outstanding job of getting tickets, they agreed. He somehow managed to secure seats for them in one of the dignitaries' boxes just above the right side of the stage, very close to the piano. They had an excellent view of the entire stage below them. Su-Li made a mental note to personally thank their new friend, Xuegin.

The first half of the performance highlighted just the symphony. It was outstanding, with compositions by Mozart and Haydn, followed by arrangements of local artists blending the sounds of traditional Chinese and western instruments! It had been a long time since she heard such musical precision. Mental snapshots of happy times wafted through Su-Li's mind as she remembered how she and Cheng listened to music together *wherever* they could find it as students without much money. Sometimes it was very good; sometimes it was not, but they always found music playing somewhere. The symphony was one of their favorites. How often they stood in line outside the hall as many students did in those days, hoping for discounted seats in the back of the theater if the performance was not a sell-out. One time they were actually given two free tickets from someone who was standing in line and became suddenly ill. They were good seats in the middle of the hall. She thought again of Cheng, his beautiful tenor voice...and fought back tears. How she wished he was here tonight – in these excellent seats, waiting for their daughter to come onto the stage.

She looked over at Qiang and saw him again as a comical toddler, learning to walk and dance at the same time. She thought of his birthday gift to her of a guitar, the broken pianos that he brought back to life, and the beautiful wooden instruments he created. She looked at her daughter-in-law, who loves music but cannot play an instrument. Guo told them she took piano lessons as a young girl, but it was during a time when pianos were being destroyed because they were considered to be evil instruments of western culture. Her lessons ended when her instructor's piano was taken away. Now, twenty years later, she is looking forward to resuming her lessons. What a wonderful wife she is for Qiang, Su-Li acknowledged. It felt good to see her son so happy!

For just a moment she remembered how music made her sad for so many years after losing her children – but not anymore!

A second piano was rolled onto the stage during intermission and placed corner to corner with the other piano.

The lights flickered – three minutes until the concert resumed. It was time. While everyone settled comfortably back into their seats, Su-Li, Qiang and Guo sat poised on the edge of theirs, looking down at the pianos.

Lights dimmed. The audience fell silent as the sound of a lone oboe echoed through the hall for musicians to retune their instruments. Clapping for the stately conductor as he reappeared onstage gave Su-Li a strangely satisfying way of releasing her tension. The conductor acknowledged the audience with a respectful bow, then spoke into the microphone.

"Honorable guests, ladies and gentlemen, it gives me great pleasure to introduce our visiting performers this evening. They represent seven countries and have traveled extensively during the past three years, sharing their musical talent with audiences all over the world. On behalf of the Peoples Republic of China, the City of Beijing, and the Beijing Symphony Orchestra, please make them welcome...Music Students International!"

Su-Li had such a huge lump in her throat she could hardly swallow as the group of ten students walked onto the stage and took their places. Emily was at the far piano and a young man at the closer one. The others sat in "V" formation at the front of the stage, four on one side and four on the other, instruments readied.

The orchestra began with the introductory piece of a four-part selection, gradually bringing the students in as the orchestra faded. Then it was all Music Students International.

They were unbelievably good! Emily's fingers flew over the keys so fast they were almost a blur. Then it was the young man's turn, followed by both playing in echo style interspersed with the other instruments. Such energy! Such talent! The music was strong, then lilting, passionate, flawlessly played.

Su-Li savored every note, every piece, every movement Emily made. Her daughter was absolutely stunning from her musical fingers to her bright red dress, with her long, silky black hair and prominent white "feather" glistening under the lights.

Oh, how she wished they could have played all night, but it ended. The audience clapped heartily. The city dignitaries in the front row stood in an official gesture of approval, which invited everyone else to stand and clap some more. They played an encore.

It was wonderful...and then it was over.

No...it wasn't! The conductor spoke again into the microphone: "Ladies and gentlemen, on behalf of the City of Beijing and our Honorable Governor, and to show appreciation for our wonderful symphony and guest musicians, you are all invited downstairs to meet and greet our performers and join them for refreshments."

Su-Li's feet felt like they were floating on air as they made their way down the winding staircase to a huge room. Symphony members mingled with the crowd while the students stood in a reception line, greeting the audience as they filed past. Su-Li, Qiang, and Guo got in line, eager to meet Emily.

Su-Li's hand trembled slightly as she extended it to the young woman she knew was her daughter and looked into her face. Her eyes were close to tears, but she fought them back. Twenty years seemed like yesterday as the mental picture of the last time she held her daughter's hand stared back at her. Once again, she didn't want to let go!

Emily looked puzzled for a moment as Su-Li held onto her hand. Then she looked at Su-Li again, closer, with eyes moving from her face to her hair! She looked over at Qiang, then to his hair...and stopped dead! She put her other hand firmly on Su-Li's arm, and the world stood still for mother and daughter. But this time, it was the daughter who would not let go!

Su-Li could not have moved out of Emily's grip even if she wanted to, but suddenly, it didn't matter...nothing else in the room mattered! She was in a pseudo world, only vaguely aware of Qiang and Guo standing motionless in back of her and people waiting in line behind them.

The spell was broken when a middle-aged woman with a shocked face rushed up from somewhere in back of Emily, staring at Su-Li while carefully pulling Emily's hands away. "Ma'am," she whispered, "would you and your party be kind enough to have some refreshments and join us again at the end of the reception hour? We would like to talk to you."

"Of course," stammered Su-Li, as her focus came back to the present."

Qiang was silent and started to steer his mother away from the reception line, but Emily grabbed his arm. She turned around, still holding onto Qiang's arm, and spoke hushed to the woman in back of her.

"Mother!"

"Yes, I know, honey. We'll talk later. Right now, you need to keep the line moving."

Emily continued to greet people, chatting and smiling graciously, occasionally looking over at Su-Li, Qiang, and Guo as they politely sipped punch and sampled cookies. Several people stopped to talk to Su-Li and Qiang, inquiring about their unique hair similarities. Were they related to the talented pianist? "Distantly," was Qiang's appropriate answer.

The crowd dissipated. The woman Emily called "mother" spoke with the other students briefly, apparently telling them to go along as they were going to stay for a while longer.

With just a handful of musicians and staff left in the room, Emily and her parents invited Su-Li, Qiang and Guo to join them at a cluster of chairs in a corner. Noise from people moving about, workers putting the room back in order, and food being put away, made private conversation difficult. When the conductor came by to bid them a good evening, Emily's mother asked if there was possibly a room where they could have a quiet meeting. It was obviously awkward for her, Su-Li realized, and offered an explanation.

"I am a music teacher," Su-Li told the conductor. "I am here at the generosity of my deceased husband's company, and on behalf of my students, several of whom show much promise to be able to do as the young people in this group are doing. I am encouraged by my husband's company to find more information about how we can establish a similar ensemble that might include some of the young music students from China."

That said it all. They were offered a complimentary meeting room to carry on their discussion. As Emily sat anxiously next to her father, "mother" wasted no time – they did not have much time!

"Are you thinking what we are thinking? Is it possible that you might be Emily's biological family? By the way, my name is Vicki and this is my husband, Gus. Please tell us your names."

Su-Li responded with similar urgency and honesty. "I am Su-Li Ming and this is my son and daughter-in-law, Qiang and Guo. And yes, I believe there is a possibility that I might be Emily's birth mother. Emily...or Xiu Su as my daughter was called, was born on February 21st, 1984."

Emily could not hold back the tears that now ran freely down her cheeks. Gus placed a comforting but protective arm around her as Guo sat on the other side, offering her tissues. Vicki's face paled, her eyes searching Su-Li's face. "We were told *that was* her birth date. Emily knows how she came to be our daughter, Su-Li. Gus and

I knew she would realize at a young age that she was not our biological child, so when she started asking questions, we told her the truth...that we were blessed to receive her from an orphanage in China, that there was no way to ever find or know about her birth parents, or even if they were alive, but we promised to love her forever as she was now our child. It is so unbelievable that this might be happening. It is only because of your hair..."

"Yes, I know," Su-Li agreed. "Emily's hair is what drew me to her picture in a travel magazine. As you can see, Qiang also shares this family trait."

They all looked over at Qiang, who remained silent. So far, his mother was doing fine.

"Would you like to see a picture of my husband? I think you will notice another similarity." She pulled Cheng's company picture from her purse. The smile spoke for itself.

There was a knock at the door, and a friendly reminder from the other side that it was almost time to lock up.

"Can we meet you somewhere tomorrow," Gus asked? "I think we need to have a little time to absorb all of this, but we certainly cannot let it end here. Emily has had so many questions that we cannot answer. We need to talk some more."

Su-Li was relieved. She wondered what would happen if they were to recognize each other. How would Emily react? How would her adoptive parents react? Now she knew. They were as shocked and curious about her family as she was about them.

Qiang took the initiative with Gus. "Guo and I live on the outskirts of Beijing; Mother is visiting us from a village north of here. After twenty years of not knowing where Xiu-Su...or Emily was, there is no way we could let it end here either. Would ten o'clock tomorrow be convenient? How can we get in touch with you?"

Gus scribbled down a hotel name and room number and handed it to Qiang. "Here's where we are staying. Just give us a call on the house phone when you get there and we will meet you in the lobby. Please join us for breakfast."

"Thank you...and here is my phone number as well," said Qiang, as he handed Gus a card.

Emily was still sitting next to Guo with the box of tissues on her lap. As they all stood to leave, Emily hugged her new family, turning first to Guo, then to Qiang and Su-Li. Then, with heart-felt sincerity, she stopped and looked intently at Su-Li.

"Thank you for coming to my concert. No matter what happens, I will never forget this night. Thank you for being here."

Emotions were running the gamut for three people trying unsuccessfully to sleep. Su-Li looked at the clock; it was 2:10 a.m. She walked into the sitting room and saw the silhouette of her son in a chair in front of the window, staring into the night toward the lights of Beijing. "Are you not able to sleep either, my son?" she asked as she lowered herself onto a sofa on the other side of the room.

He turned around to face her in the darkened room. "No, Mother, there is too much on my mind. How about you? Are you excited...or nervous about finding Emily?"

"Both, but I did not anticipate the concerns that would come with it. This whole situation is so complicated that my head is spinning, worrying about tomorrow. There is absolutely no doubt in my mind that Emily is my daughter – your sister, but as Vicki and Gus pointed out, she has a lot of questions. It is understandable that she wants to know who she is, where she was born, and who we are, but I am worried about how much we will truthfully be able to tell her."

"I am having those thoughts and others, Mother. I could not have imagined, after learning about the caution taken to protect our endangered children, that there would ever be a chance of finding Syaran or Xiu-Su. The trail is supposed to be covered completely. Now, here we are on the threshold of something that is not supposed to be possible, and with serious implications. It could be disastrous to react with human emotions, say something we shouldn't, and have our whole operation come crashing down – not just on our end, but on the adoptive parents' end as well. Even though caution is not needed as much today as in the past, as we have abandoned the cave, we could still put a lot of people's lives in jeopardy if we are not careful."

There was pensive silence, finally broken by the shuffle of quiet footsteps as Guo entered the room and joined Su-Li on the sofa.

"Welcome to our gathering of insomniacs," Qiang chided. The bit of laughter felt good, lifting the cloud of concern, albeit briefly. "And how are *you* feeling about tomorrow? Are you also thinking about what we can and cannot say?"

Guo was silent for a few moments. "Yes, I am concerned about how we will answer the questions I am sure Vicki and Gus and Emily will be asking, but have decided not to dwell on it. Do you remember a lesson from our Bible class a few weeks ago about not worrying if a time comes for you to speak and you don't know what you should say? Our teacher said something like: Don't worry about what you will do or say when a crisis comes into your life. You will know what to do and be given the right words at the right time. Maybe we should believe in that message and not worry so much."

"Thank you for reminding me about that lesson, my wise wife. I'm counting on it being true because if Emily is my sister, and I honestly believe that she is, my instinct is that I just want to tell her the truth, scoop her up and take her home with us. But that would be selfish. Even if she *wanted* to come with us – to return to her roots so to speak, it would be devastating for Vicki and Gus who raised her for twenty years. No, she does not belong in our country – in our world. She belongs right where she is – in the world she has always known; in her place of good education, music, freedom, and opportunities."

After a few seconds, he added: "Even though she "is ours," she is not one of us. She never can be!"

Qiang's words stung Su-Li's heart. After twenty years of wondering, wishing and wanting to know her daughter, the naked truth hurt. They could never be a "family" – ever. They were a world apart.

As soon as he spoke, Qiang realized the pain his words must have caused his mother. "Please forgive me, Mother. I didn't mean to speak those words harshly. I am speaking with both my head and my heart. I am sorry."

Su-Li was thankful for the darkness, the silence of tears, and the hand of her daughter-in-law as it reached over to her arm. Her voice was raspy as she replied to her son: "Your spoken thoughts are the same as my quiet ones, Qiang, and in a strange way, hearing you say them out loud helps me accept the truth.

"Ever since I found out that Syaran and Xiu-Su were alive, I believed that, if by some miracle I should ever find either or both of them, I would hang onto them forever and never let go, even if it meant my death. But it is different now, at least with Xiu-Su. Even though she is an adult, it is not her will nor mine...or yours that will make the determination. It is the time in which we live and the circumstances that pulled us apart. We are in different countries with different governments, different ways of living, different customs, different...everything."

They sat in silence until Qiang spoke again, this time *from his heart,* audibly sniffing back invisible tears. His voice sounded sad, frustrated, angry, almost desperate.

"And what are we supposed to do?! – Never see her again? Never call her, send messages on the computer, write letters, or wish her a happy birthday because we are being monitored? Are we supposed to just forget about her forever because we exist under a constant veil of suspicion? Why?! Why can't she know the truth – the rest of the world does! Why would God bring us together after all these years just to tear us apart again?"

Somehow…Su-Li knew the words to say to her grieving son. They just came spilling out: "My son, we have been given a glimpse into a world outside of our own, through a window that was *supposed* to be closed. I believe we have received an unexpected blessing from a gracious and sympathetic God who has heard our prayers. Do you remember your own words that night when you and your father insisted I go to the mission church with you to meet Roberto, the new leader? I didn't want to go, especially after you told me he was going to deliver a message about our forbidden children and "hope," which was something I did not have. Against my will, I grudgingly went with you. Roberto's message changed my life. It pulled me out of the darkness so I could live a new life. Now listen to the words of your mother…perhaps you need to remember what hope is all about. God <u>has</u> brought us together for a reason, and I truly believe that. We may never know what the reason is, but we need to trust His timing, His wisdom, and do His will, wherever it leads us.

223

"I also believe with all my heart that we <u>will</u> see Emily again...but probably not for a while. I sincerely doubt that she will leave China and not want to reconnect with us at some time in the future."

There. She didn't know where those meaningful words came from, but they impressed even her. They sat through another period of silence, followed by a big sigh and a chuckle from the silhouette in the window. "You are right, Mother...I am in the presence of two wise women tonight, for which I am thankful. Why do I have such a hard time taking my own advice about who is in charge...and it is not me! None of what is happening is because of any of us. So why don't we all just wait and see what tomorrow brings? It should be an interesting day!"

Qiang's normal voice was back, along with a big yawn, reminding them of the time.

With handshakes and hugs, the two families greeted each other in the hotel lobby and followed the newly-reunited brother and sister to the breakfast lounge. *How different everyone looks this morning,* thought Su-Li as she noted the casual shirts, jeans, and sneakers of the young adults. Vicki and Gus sported American-style casual clothes, while she wore the only other clothes she brought with her – a loose-fitting dress and her comfortable "teaching" shoes. One thing they did have in common, however – they were all very hungry!

Su-Li was surprised to see Vicki, Gus, and Emily also drinking tea in the morning. She learned it was a Canadian custom as well as Chinese. But no amount of tea could erase the tired looking faces around the table. Obviously, she and Qiang and Guo were not the only ones suffering from lack of sleep!

Guo sat across the table from Qiang, thoughtfully allowing her husband to have the seat next to his sister, occasionally joining them in laughter as they compared footwear, and in seriousness as they talked about pianos. It saddened Su-Li as she watched her son and daughter, knowing they would only be together for a short time...at least for now.

After an ample breakfast buffet, it was time for serious talk. Vicki and Gus motioned for Emily to come over and sit between them so she could hear better and everyone could hear her.

"Su-Li," Gus began, "tell us about yourself and Cheng. We know that Emily wants to know as much as possible about her biological parents, and so do we. By the way, we <u>are</u> convinced that you are her biological family, and I think you believe that as well – correct?"

"Yes," replied Su-Li., as she looked over at Emily. We have been thinking about that possibility for months when pictures and information about Emily were provided by a friend of ours. After last night, we are convinced she is our Xiu-Su."

The beginning of the conversation was devoted to Su-Li's and Cheng's backgrounds – where they were born, their family and education, where they lived since being married, Cheng's passing, and Su-Li's current occupation as a music teacher. She spoke nothing of children except to mention when Qiang was born. Vicki wrote everything down, asking for spellings, and noting dates. Emily listened intently as she heard about her biological family for the first time, asking questions, including one about her paternal and maternal grandparents – did any of them have their hair feature?

"I vaguely remember my mother's father having a rather jagged looking swatch of white hair on both sides of his head," replied Su-Li. "He died when I was very young, so I don't remember much about him."

Emily asked several times for clarification regarding Chinese "tradition" that she did not understand. Guo proved to be the expert in that category as her recent studies included Chinese history and culture from ancient to modern times, giving fascinating insight into her country's traditions and beliefs.

Gus continued with another request: "Please tell us what you know...*what you remember* about Emily."

There it was – the question she knew would come but didn't know how to answer. She felt her throat close and tears welling up as she tried to talk. Qiang looked at his mother and knew it was time for him to speak. "Let me help with that answer, Gus. I am sure you all know about the one-child-per-family policy in effect in our country. It is widely known. Many within our country are convinced that it is a good thing, a necessary thing, to control our over-population problem. That may be true in theory, but in reality, it is not working and is painful for those who have been affected by it as our family has."

Then Qiang focused squarely on Emily and continued: "Being forced to give you up at birth, Emily, has haunted my mother for over twenty years. As you have probably just realized, it is painful for her yet today. I am going to be very truthful with you. You have another brother who was taken away four years before you, even though his birth was only two months after the edict went into effect. You are 20 years old; I am 28; Syaran is 24. We do not know where he is and probably never will, although we believe he was adopted by a family within China. So, my mother has dealt with her grief twice. She only had a few minutes to get to know you and give you the name of Xiu-Su which, by the way, means 'beautiful and unadorned,' before you were taken away. My mother, father, and I knew nothing more."

There was silence as everyone looked at Emily, waiting for a response. "Who took us – the government?" she asked.

"That is a difficult question to answer, Emily," Qiang replied. "The one-child-per-family mandate is a law of our government, but you and Syaran were taken by different people. Syaran was supposedly taken by hospital workers and delivered to an orphanage. You were taken by a man who lived in our village – a man who many people believe worked for the government, but it was not determined for sure. He was just the person who took the forbidden children. Few people ever spoke to him because of what he did, so very few knew anything about him or what connection he had with the government. He died about ten years ago but, of course, was replaced by another man, similarly rejected by people in the village."

Su-Li slowly regained her composure, relieved and thankful for the honest answers from her son.

"I'm sorry, Su-Li," said Gus. "I didn't mean to upset you and apologize for being so forward. Vicki has told me more than once that I tend to be like a big bear charging through the woods. It's just that for twenty years we have wondered about many things, never thinking we would ever have a chance to talk to you personally."

"I understand, and of course you want to know. I would also if I were you, and we will try our best to answer. But also, please tell us about Emily."

For the next twenty minutes, Emily was in the spotlight...her years as a baby, a toddler, a youngster, and a teenager. Vicki and Gus pulled out their wallets and shared a collection of pictures – pictures Su-Li silently wished she could have, but dared not ask for.

"Here, Su-Li. This is Emily's high school graduation picture. We have more at home. Would you like to have it?"

That lump in her throat was back again as she accepted the small picture of Emily. "Thank you, Vicki. This is a precious gift."

Su-Li and Qiang were especially interested to hear Vicki's story of their common distinctive hair marking: "When Emily's hair started growing in, we were curious of course about the swatch of white hair. We initially thought she might have been injured at one time and the hair follicles in that spot damaged, but when I took her to the salon to have her hair cut for the first time, I was told that our theory was not necessarily correct. Yes, *it could be*, I was told, but it could also be inherited. It would not even have to be from female to female, it could be inherited from a father as well. I've had a premonition ever since then, of seeing a picture of a Chinese man or woman with such a mark. It would come to mind even when I saw a person with naturally graying or salt and pepper hair that often starts on the side. That was why we all looked so surprised when you appeared in the reception line with the perfect replica of Emily's hair. Seeing Qiang was a double shock. When you knew Emily's birthdate, there was no more doubt that you were Emily's birth family.

"By the way, Su-Li," Vicki continued, "are you or anyone in your family musically gifted like Emily is? You mentioned you are a music teacher."

"Well, I don't know about being gifted," Su-Li replied, "but music has always been a special enjoyment for our family. I grew up playing the traditional Chinese instruments like my mother played – the pipa, erhu, and chimes, although I never had lessons. I just figured them out by listening to my mother and practicing. That is how I also learned to play the American guitar that Qiang gave me a few years ago for my birthday – lots of practicing. I did learn how to read music at the university, but forgot most of it until just a few years ago when I had a real desire to learn to play the piano. Thanks to a patient music teacher in our church, I 'relearned' reading music, which helped me play the piano correctly so I could teach it to my students.

"Cheng did not play any instruments, but he had a beautiful voice and loved to sing. Qiang takes after his father with singing and also has a unique special gift of his own in creating and repairing musical instruments. He has a studio not far from here where he brings instruments back to life and builds new ones that he sells through catalogs. But tell us - how did Emily get started with her wonderful music?"

"We knew she was musically gifted," Vicki said proudly, "when she was four years old and crawled up on the piano bench next to me. I showed her how I was making the music and she surprised Gus and me both when she poked around and found the same note I was playing an octave higher. Every time I played a note, she played the same one higher. We knew then that she had a natural ear for music and decided to give her piano lessons. We had a hard time finding a piano teacher who was willing to accept a four-year-old, but we eventually found one. She took to it like a duck to water. She was even creating her own songs by the time she was eight."

"Being awarded a music scholarship didn't hurt, either," Gus added with a smile. "Not only did she earn a full scholarship, but it included all of her expenses paid while she travels with this group of students on behalf of her school. Of course, it costs Vicki and me a small fortune to go along with her, but we wouldn't have it any other way. We could not deny her this wonderful opportunity." He beamed a parental smile over at Emily, who accepted the attention with low-key acknowledgment.

"We haven't mentioned it," added Vicki, "but Emily is our only child and to say that we are proud of her would be an understatement."

Su-Li was thankful for the short time of reflection and silence that followed so she could force herself to rise above the resentment she was feeling of being denied the parental right to her child. Why had someone else been given the privilege of loving and caring for her beautiful daughter? Why couldn't she have been the one to teach her music? It was tough to have to accept the words of wisdom she gave to her son last night: that being with Emily for even a short time was a blessing they were never supposed to have and that they needed to be thankful for the unexpected window. It was difficult.

"Su-Li...mother," said Emily quietly, looking at both women, first at Su-Li, then at Vicki, then back at Su-Li in confusion. "What should I call you?"

Everyone froze. It was a simple and innocent question, but no one wanted to answer or even offer a suggestion. Su-Li struggled to put her mind back on track and speak convincingly. "My husband called me Su-Li Pu, Emily, or sometimes just Pu. In Chinese, Pu means feather. Very appropriate, don't you think?" she asked, smiling at her look-alike daughter. "Why don't you just call me Su-Li Pu. It is a special name that I miss hearing."

Su-Li saw the anxiety on the faces of Vicki and Gus relax. She knew she had just removed herself as a threat to their identity as Emily's parents. Yes, it was the right thing for her to do...but it hurt.

"Su-Li Pu," Emily continued, "I have read a lot on the internet about China's one-child policy and I know about the fate of the girl babies. Did you think I was going to be killed when I was taken from you? How did I escape that fate? I am just curious about how I got here. I know now that I was pulled away from parents who wanted me and delivered to other parents who wanted me, but how did I escape the fate that happened to all those thousands of other girls?"

Now was when she knew she had to be really careful and did not have to be reminded by Guo's gentle nudge against her arm. She also recognized that Emily knew more about the one-child edict than she had anticipated. But *somehow*, she had to speak the truth. ***"God, please give me the words,"*** she prayed silently.

She started cautiously. "Yes, Emily, I was well aware of the fact that if you were a girl your life would be in danger. In all honesty, I prayed that you would be a boy so you would have a better chance to survive and be adopted. Even though the official policy was to assure parents that their daughters would be taken to an orphanage and receive good care until they were adopted, I did not believe it in my heart. When you were born, I feared instantly for your life. All I remember was hanging onto you with every bit of strength I had until you were forcefully pried out of my arms and then collapsing on the floor. I have been told that I was feverish for days and, truthfully, I don't remember anything more. I knew nothing about where you were taken or how.

"What I did come to believe many years later, however, thanks to a missionary family, was that Heaven is for real. It is a place where families are reunited. I was told that all those we have loved in our lives and have gone on before us will be waiting to greet us when we arrive. We will know each other and live in a beautiful place of peace and happiness for eternity. So, I knew that if you had died, you would know that I loved you. And I believe right now that

232

Cheng is in Heaven, waiting for the rest of his family. We will all be together again someday, perhaps not as a biological family, but as a family united within our hearts. Learning about the promise of Heaven has lifted me out of devastation and has brought me great comfort.

"So no, I do not know the road you traveled to escape the fate of the other baby girls except it is my belief you were spared because God had plans for you. There is something you are meant to do in your life. Maybe it is with your music. Or maybe it was to fill a hole in the hearts of Vicki and Gus who must have prayed for a beautiful little girl just like you that they could love and raise as their own. Whatever it was, or is, it meant you had to survive and you did. None of us here had any control over your journey. You were in God's hands and He took care of you. That is the best way I can answer your question."

No one wanted to break the silence that lingered after the beautiful, heart-felt explanation Su-Li gave her daughter. Vicki reached over and put an arm around a tearful Emily, with the comfort of the mother Su-Li wished she could have been. It was bitter sweet, but she knew she said what had to be said, as painful as it was for everyone...including herself.

Emily wiped away her tears, rose, and walked around the table to Su-Li. Taking her hands, she gently pulled her up from her chair. It was an indescribably wonderful moment in Su-Li's life as her daughter held her close and whispered quietly, "Thank you Mother. I love you." It was a moment of tear-filled emotion, mixed with joy...and closure.

###

The two families from opposite sides of the world exchanged phone numbers, mailing addresses, and email addresses, expressing hope that someday they would be able to communicate freely and maybe even visit again in person. It was time to leave, but the air was electrically charged – no one wanted to be the first to say good-bye. Hearts were silently breaking and it was obvious that Emily was still close to tears, as was Su-Li. Qiang was quiet, but his pensive mood spoke of sadness as he and Guo followed the group down the hallway into the lobby.

Guo, the only "extended" family member, decided to take charge of "what's next." She looked over at Gus, Vicki, and Emily as they stood together in the lobby and asked: "When do you have to leave for the airport? Do you have some time for us to introduce you to an authentic Chinese tradition?"

"Yes, we do, Guo, and we would love to," replied Vicki. "We need to check out of our hotel room and put our luggage into the holding area, but our transport won't be picking us up for almost three hours. We can be checked out and back down to the lobby in probably fifteen or twenty minutes if you don't mind waiting."

"We don't mind at all. We will meet you back here when you are ready."

Emily's face lit up with "Cheng's beautiful smile" as she rushed off with Vicki and Gus to pack. "We'll be right back," she promised, peering out of the elevator as the door closed.

"And what do you have in mind, my enterprising and sometimes mischievous wife?" asked Qiang. "I have seen that look before."

Guo smiled. "I think there are several shoe stores within walking distance from here where we can treat each member of our Canadian family to a new pair of shoes. Perhaps the three of us could use a new pair, too. The river is just a few blocks away."

They knew exactly what Guo was talking about. "Yes! What a wonderful idea, Guo," said a thankful Su-Li. "Maybe it will bring peace for all of us, especially Emily. We must remember that we were prepared. We knew about her for months, but she has only known us and her real identity for a day. She needs time."

It was a warm, hazy day as the group of six emerged from the hotel and headed for the stores across the street. They browsed, laughed, and savored every minute of what they knew might be their last time together for quite a while. But it was alright. Everything was as it should be...***as it had to be***.

"There's one more store over here that we have to visit," said Guo, as she pointed to a trendy shoe store. "We want to buy each of you a new pair of shoes."

"Why?" said Vicki. "What's wrong with our shoes?"

"Nothing. It's just part of the Chinese custom I was talking about. Then we are going for a walk down by the river."

"Oh."

As they filed out of the store, each carrying their new shoes in a bag and started walking toward the river, Emily's surprised voice could be heard above the bustle of the street...

...We are going to do <u>what </u>with our old shoes?!!

Su-Li smiled as they all took turns tossing their shoes into the river. *Will Emily ever understand the <u>true</u> significance of this old tradition,* she wondered? *Will we someday be able to tell her the whole truth about the lives that Guang and Qiang saved? Will my daughter ever be able to see the imprint of her own tiny foot on the cave wall?*

Maybe. But for now, six people put new shoes on their feet and looked to the future, wherever it would lead them.

About the Author

Madelyn Rohrer

Born in Upstate New York, Madelyn grew up as a "border kid." She spent early years living on both sides of the Canadian border and later years in Southern California where she lived just a few miles from the Mexican border.

In between borders, she spent over two decades in Jonesborough, Tennessee, the home of international storytelling, before returning to her home town in New York.

Her lifelong business career is just as diverse. It includes twenty-eight years in a large New York photographic corporation, partnership in a family-owned business, and owning her own office management company.

Madelyn's tenure in Jonesborough sparked an interest that led to yet another career—professional storyteller, speaker, and published author. Although her portfolio of oral and written stories is diverse, her favorites are those that inspire, strengthen moral values, and bring history to life. Her stories are suitable for all audiences.

Madelyn's Books

Her first book, **_Tiggy Touch Wood_**, was published in 2014 and includes ten original short stories composed for the storytelling stage and subsequently converted to written form. The book has received excellent reviews from the storytelling and literary communities, including a five-star award from Red City Review. Several stories have been chosen for writers' guild anthologies.

Shoes in the River, a novel, was released in 2015. It presents an insight into real life in China as affected by the one-child-per-family edict, which produced a world-wide dilemma still being dealt with today. The characters are fictional but the issues are real. It has received excellent reviews from Red City Review and Writers Digest.

The Ugly Popcorn Tree (2018) is a novella of true-to-life fiction concerning older orphans ("tweens"), some of the circumstances that would have them lingering in an orphanage at an older age, and the difficulties they encounter while waiting for their new homes and parents.

***Touched by Tennessee**, Second Edition*
(copyright 2016; second edition 2020) is a
collection of eight true short stories, originally
told on stage with the common thread of the
State of Tennessee. One of the stories was
chosen as a first-place winner by *Storytelling
World Awards*, a publication of the National
Storytelling Network. It is also available as an
audio book.

Children's Books

Hobie the Christmas Spider (2017) is the
first in "The Critter Series" of children's books.
It is created from a bit of Germanic folklore
and an Old-World Tradition of sharing
Christmas Eve with the animals...only from
the perspective of the spiders. It teaches
children about the love Jesus has for all living
creatures, even the tiniest of all. It is a story of
the "magic" of Christmas.

Bert the Owl Bat (2019) is the second in "The
Critter Series" of children's books. Join Bert as
he meets a new but unlikely (and scary)
friend quite by chance. Bert and his friend are
leery of each other at first but soon decide in
their minds to be friends. When their lives are
interrupted by danger, their bond of
friendship becomes one of the heart.

Other Publications

Johnny Come Back (2018) is a true story of an East Tennessee couple. When Claudia, a seasoned emergency room nurse, takes her husband to the hospital on Christmas Eve 2017 with flu-like symptoms, they don't return home for eighty-four days. This is their amazing story as they lived it. (Written for them by Madelyn Rohrer).

Coming Soon:

There's a Ferret in the Neighborhood! The third children's book in The Critter Series.

Children of the Edict – Sequel to ***Shoes in the River.***

For more information on any of Madelyn's books, including available formats and how to order, log onto her website at: **www.storytellermadelynrohrer.com**

...or visit her YouTube channel at www.YouTube.com and search for: ***Stories by Madelyn Rohrer.***

Bibliography

Historical facts and information are from multiple internet sources, including:

One-Child-Per-Family Policy
Washingtonpost.com/world/asia_pacific/one-is-enough-chinese-families-lukewarm-over-easing-of-one-child-policy/2015/01/22/bdfeff1e-9d7e-11e4-86a3-1b56

Newsweek.com/2014/01/24/one-child-policy-one-big-problem-china-245118.html

BBC.com/news/world-asia-china-2553339   28 December 2013

NYTimes.com/2013/05/22/opinion/chinas-brutal-one-child-policy-.html

Britannica.com/topic/one-child-policy

Religion in China
Council on Foreign Relations: cfs.org/china/religion-china/p16272 "Religion in China," author: Eleanor Albert, Online Writer/Editor, Updated June 10, 2015

Economist.com/news/briefing/21629218.rapid-spread-christianity-forcing-official-rethink-religion-cracks

Religionfacts.com/chinese-religion

Billionbibles.org/china/three-self-church.html

Electricity in China
Cambridgeeeprg.com/wp-content/uploads/2008/11/eprg0517.pdf

Theenergycollective.com/michael-davidson/335271/china-s-electricity-sector-glance-2013

Telephones in China
Chinaunique.com/business/communic.htm

Indexmundi.com/china/telephone_system.html   "China Telephone System" Updated as of 2014

Internet in China
Firstmonday.orgojs/index.php/fm/article/view/3767/3144   "Home Computer Ownership and Internet Use in China: Trends, disparities, socioeconomic impacts, and policy implications" by Qingbin Wang and Minghao Li   6 February 2012

Pianos and Musical Instruments in China
people.wku.edu/haiwang.yuan/China/.../chinesecultureandcustoms.rtf

Miscellaneous
Chinesecultureandcustoms.com

www.ingramcontent.com/pod-product-compliance
Lightning Source LLC
Chambersburg PA
CBHW020755250626
47155CB00003B/1077